"This just isn't my day," Lean muttered and, acting on instinct, she shouldered the rifle and fired

The first blast cratered the ground a foot in front of him. He didn't flinch. The second landed square between his boots. Still, he kept coming.

He hit the porch steps two at a time. Not hesitating, he grabbed the barrel of the rifle and yanked it from her grasp, tossing it aside.

"You never were much of a shot," he said. And then he kissed her.

Dear Reader,

As a romance author, I've always been fascinated to learn how couples first met. Perhaps that's why one of the most enjoyable parts of writing a book is describing that electric moment when the hero and heroine first come into contact—their reactions, their thoughts and feelings, the emotions they experience. And for every book, just as for every couple, it's different.

In the *Sealed with a Kiss* series, the couples are brought together through the written word. For Leah and Hunter in *Mail-Order Bridegroom*, it's in the form of a newspaper advertisement. She needs a husband and he needs... Well, that changes through the course of the story, and through the course of their marriage.

I will tell you that writing this book gave me the opportunity to explore a story with greater emotional depth, a story with an incredibly strong hero and a feisty, independent heroine—a couple who in the spirit of today's Harlequin Romances "Dare to Dream"...and dare to succeed.

Yours sincerely,

Day Leclaire

MAIL-ORDER BRIDEGROOM
Day Leclaire

Harlequin Books

TORONTO • NEW YORK • LONDON
AMSTERDAM • PARIS • SYDNEY • HAMBURG
STOCKHOLM • ATHENS • TOKYO • MILAN
MADRID • WARSAW • BUDAPEST • AUCKLAND

My special thanks to Kevin Anderson for explaining
which is the serious end of a rifle. And my special,
special thanks to Sandra Marton…just for being there.
Thank you.

ISBN 0-373-03361-3

MAIL-ORDER BRIDEGROOM

Copyright © 1995 by Day Totton Smith.

First North American Publication 1995.

Printed in U.S.A.

PROLOGUE

Husband Wanted!

Woman rancher in immediate and desperate need of a man! Interested applicants should:
1. Be 25-45 years of age and looking for a permanent relationship—a kind and gentle personality is a plus!
2. Have extensive ranching background—be able to sit a horse, deal fairly with employees, herd cattle, etc.
3. Have solid business know-how—particularly the type necessary to please a bullheaded banker.

I am a twenty-six-year-old woman and can offer you a comfortable home, three square meals and some of the most beautiful scenery in Texas Hill Country. (Details of a more personal nature are open to negotiation.) Interested parties should send a letter of introduction, a resumé and references to 'Miss Bluebonnet', Box 42, Crossroads, Texas.

HUNTER PRYDE picked up the newspaper ad and reread it, a remorseless smile edging his mouth. So Leah was in 'desperate need' of a husband. How interesting. How very, very interesting...

CHAPTER ONE

'THIS will be a real marriage, right?' the applicant interrupted. 'I cain't take over the place 'lessen it's a real marriage.'

Leah glanced up from the resumé of one Titus T. Culpepper and regarded the man in question with a cool gaze. 'Could you by any chance be referring to your conjugal rights, Mr Culpepper?'

'If that means us sleepin' together, then that's what I'm referring to. Hell, yes, I mean conjugal rights.' He rocked his chair back on to two legs, her grandmother's precious Chippendale groaning beneath his bulky frame. 'You're a fine-looking woman, Miz Hampton. Always was partial to blue-eyed blondes.'

She stiffened, struggling to hide her distaste. 'I'm...flattered, but——'

'Like a bit of sweet-talk, do you?' He offered a toothy grin. 'So long as it'll get me what I want, I don't mind. Because as far as I'm concerned there's not much point in gettin' hitched if we ain't gonna share a bed.'.

'I think any discussion about rights—conjugal or otherwise—is a trifle premature at this point,' she informed him shortly. Especially when she intended to find a nice, tame husband, willing to agree to a safe, platonic relationship. One brief, youthful brush with the more volatile type of emotions had been quite sufficient. 'About your resumé, Mr Culpepper——'

'Titus T.'

'Pardon me?'

'Most folks call me Titus T. If'n we're to be wed, you might as well get used to calling me by my proper name.' He winked.

'I see.' Leah glanced at the papers before her with a jaundiced eye. This interview was definitely not turning out as she'd hoped. Unfortunately she'd already eliminated all the other applicants, except Titus T. and one other—H.P. Smith, her final interview of the day. She didn't have any choice but to give Mr Culpepper a fair and thorough hearing. 'It says here that you have extensive ranching experience.'

'Fact is, it was a farm I ran. But ranch...farm.' He shrugged. 'Same difference. So long's I can tell which end of a cow to stick the bucket under it don't matter, right?'

She stared, appalled. 'Actually, it does.'

'Not to my way of thinking.' Before she had a chance to argue the point he leaned forward, studying her intently. 'Your ad also says you need a businessman. Why's that?'

He'd hit on the main reason for her ad. While she could run a ranch with no problem, she needed a husband well-skilled in business to handle her financial obligations. Leah hesitated, reluctant to explain the precariousness of her monetary situation, but knowing she didn't have much choice.

'The ranch is experiencing financial difficulties,' she admitted. 'In all honesty, we face bankruptcy if I can't obtain a loan. Our banker suggested that if I were married to an experienced rancher who had a strong business background they'd be willing to make that loan. That's why I placed the ad.'

Titus T. nodded, a thoughtful frown creasing his brow. 'I can understand a sweet thing like you having trouble with ciphering, so I'd be more than happy to keep track of the money for you.' An expansive smile slid across his face. 'Matter of fact, it might be a good idea to put all the accounts and such in my name for safekeeping. Then I'll talk the bank into giving us a nice fat loan. Don't you worry your head none about that.'

Leah fought to conceal her horror. There wasn't any point in continuing the interview. She knew a con-man when she met one. How had she managed to get herself into this predicament? She should have found some excuse the minute he opened his mouth. If she hadn't been so desperate, she would have. Determined to tread warily, she inclined her head, as though she found his every word to be perfectly acceptable.

'Of course. I don't see any problem with that,' she lied without a qualm, and stood, brushing her waist-length braid back over her shoulder. 'But I'm afraid our time is up. My next appointment is due any minute.' She could only pray that the final applicant would prove more suitable. The alternatives were unthinkable.

'Now, Miz Hampton...'

'I appreciate your coming,' she said, not giving him an opportunity to debate the issue. Loath as she was to come out from behind the protection of her father's huge oak desk, she wanted Titus T. Culpepper out of her study and on his way. Heading for the door, she kept a wary eye on him, hoping it wouldn't be necessary to call for Patrick, her foreman. 'I'll be making my decision in the next few days and will let you know.'

A trifle reluctantly he gained his feet and approached. 'You best think about one more thing afore you make that decision.'

She never saw it coming. Moving with amazing speed for a man of his size, he closed the distance separating them and snatched her into his arms. She turned her head just in time, his clumsy attempt at a kiss landing on her cheek instead of her mouth.

'Come on, sweetpea,' he growled, tightening his hold. 'How're you gonna know what sort of husband I'd be without a smooch or two?'

'Let go of me!'

Thoroughly disgusted and more than a little frightened, she fought his hold with a desperation that must have taken him by surprise, for his grip slackened just enough for her to wriggle out of his embrace. Taking instant advantage, Leah bolted across the room to the gun-rack. Snatching free her rifle, she rammed several slugs into the magazine and confronted Titus T.

'Time to leave, Mr Culpepper. And I do mean now,' she announced in a furious voice, giving him a brisk poke in the gut with the barrel of the rifle.

To her relief, he didn't require any further encouragement. His hands shot into the air and he took a hasty step backward. 'Now, Miz Hampton,' he protested. 'No need to get yourself in an uproar. It were jez a kiss. If we're to be wed——'

'I think you can forget that idea,' she cut in with conviction. Wisps of silver-blonde hair drifted into her eyes, but she didn't dare release her grip on the rifle long enough to push them back.

He glared in outrage. 'You sayin' no because of a little bitty kiss? Unless you marry a mouse, any man worthy of the name's gonna want a hell of a lot more from you than that.'

She refused to debate the point...especially when she'd lose the argument. It was the one detail in this whole crazy scheme that she preferred not to dwell on. 'It's not your problem, Mr Culpepper, since you won't be that man.'

'Damned tootin'.' He reached out and snatched a battered hat from off the rack by the study door. 'Don't know why you put an ad in the paper, if'n you didn't want a real husband. False advertising, that's what I call it.'

He stomped from the room and Leah followed, still carrying the rifle. No point in taking unnecessary risks. If nothing else, it would give Titus T. pause should he decide to turn amorous again. She needn't have worried. Without another word, he marched across the front porch and down the steps. Climbing into his battered flatbed truck, he slammed the rusty door closed. A minute later he disappeared down the drive.

Watching him leave, Leah's shoulders sagged. 'I must have been crazy to believe this would work,' she muttered, rubbing a weary hand across her brow. 'What am I doing?'

But she knew the answer to that. She was doing exactly what her father would have wanted her to do when faced with a buy-out attempt from one of the largest and most ruthless companies in the state: protecting the ranch and her grandmother by marrying. While every last ranch in the area had caved in to Lyon Enterprises' ruthless tactics and sold their property, Hampton Homestead remained firm. Even completely surrounded by the 'enemy', they refused to sell, no matter what.

Of course, there had been no other choice but to defy Lyon. For, as much as the ranch meant to Leah, it meant even more to Grandmother Rose. And Leah would do anything for her grandmother. Anything. Even stand up to a huge, ruthless company against overwhelming odds. Even offer herself in marriage in order to get the money necessary to win their fight.

'We're not selling the place; I don't care what dirty tricks they pull,' the elderly woman had announced just that morning, after the latest offer from Lyon Enterprises had arrived. 'The only way they'll get me out of here is in a pine box! My grandfather died fighting for this land. So did my father. And so will I, if that's what it comes to.'

Then she'd crossed her skinny arms across her non-existent bosom, stuck her chin in the air and squeezed her eyes closed, as though waiting for the undertaker to arrive.

But Leah had believed her. If the ranch went bankrupt and they were forced off the land, it would kill her grandmother. It was that simple. Keeping the ranch in the family was essential, which meant finding a solution to their current predicament. The problem was, unless she found a way to pry some money from the local bank, losing the ranch would soon be inevitable.

It had taken three long years of arguing to realize that the bank wouldn't loan money to a single woman in her mid-twenties. They'd proven especially reluctant when they'd discovered that she alone shouldered the financial burden of an elderly grandmother and a ranch full of human and animal 'lame ducks'. Learning of this year's running battle to prevent a take-over bid from one of the most powerful companies in the state gave them the best excuse of all to refuse any aid.

On the other hand, she'd recently been told that lending money to a family whose male head consisted in equal parts of a businessman and a rancher was a different proposition altogether. And, though she didn't fully understand why that should matter, it provided the loophole for which she'd been so desperately searching.

She took instant advantage. She immediately set out to find herself just such a husband, even if it meant putting an ad in the paper and offering herself to the highest bidder. She frowned, thinking of Titus T. Unfortunately, she wouldn't be offering herself to any of the applicants she'd interviewed to date.

What she really needed was a knight in shining armor to come riding up her drive, ready and able to slay all her dragons. A foolish wish, she knew. But still... Some silly, romantic part of her couldn't help dreaming for the impossible.

Leah glanced at her watch. Her final interview should arrive any time. She could only hope that he'd prove more acceptable than the others—docile enough to agree to all her demands and yet skilled enough in business matters to satisfy the bank. As though in response to her silent wish, a solitary rider appeared over a low ridge, shadowed black against the burnt-orange glow of a low-hanging sun. She shaded her eyes and studied him with keen curiosity. Could this be H.P. Smith, her final applicant?

He rode easily, at home in the saddle, swaying with a natural, effortless rhythm. Even from a distance she could tell that his horse was a beauty—the pale tan coat without a blemish, the ebony mane and tail gleaming beneath the golden rays of a setting sun. The animal was also a handful. But a handful he mastered without difficulty.

She frowned, something about him bothering her. If only she could figure out what. Then it hit her. She knew the man. On some basic, intuitive level she recognized the way he sat his horse, the simple, decisive manner with which he controlled the animal, the square, authoritative set of his shoulders. Even the angle of his hat was faintly familiar.

But who the hell was he?

She waited and watched, intent on the stranger's every movement. He rode into the yard as though he owned the place... as though he were lord here and her purpose in life was to cater to his every pleasure. From beneath the brim of his hat Leah caught a glimpse of jet-black hair and deep-set, watchful eyes, his shadowed features taut and angled, as though hewn from granite. Then he dismounted, tying his buckskin to the hitching post. Not giving the vaguest acknowledgement, he turned to cross the yard toward her.

He stripped his gloves from his hands as he came, tucking them into his belt, and she found herself staring at those hands, at the strength and power conveyed by his loosely held fists. She knew those hands... But where? A flash of memory hit her—the gentle sweep of callused fingers against her breasts, tender and yet forceful, pain mixed with ecstasy—and she gasped.

And that was when he looked up.

Full sunlight cast the shadow from his face and re-vealed to her the threat—and the promise—in his cold black eyes. In that instant she realized who he was, and why he'd come.

'This just isn't my day,' she muttered and, acting on blind instinct, shouldered her rifle and fired.

The first blast cratered the ground a foot in front of him. He didn't flinch. He didn't even break stride. He came at her, his steady gaze fixed firmly on her face. She jacked out the shell and pumped another into the chamber. The second blast landed square between his boots, showering the black leather with dirt and debris. Still he kept coming, faster now, hard-packed muscle moving with cat-like speed. She wasn't given the op-portunity to get off another round.

He hit the porch steps two at a time. Not hesitating a moment, he grabbed the barrel of the rifle and yanked it from her grasp, tossing it aside. His hands landed heavily on her shoulder, catapulting her straight into his arms. With a muffled shriek, she grabbed a fistful of shirt to keep from falling.

'You never were much of a shot,' he said, his voice low and rough. And then he kissed her.

His kiss was everything she remembered and more. He'd always combined strength with tenderness, but now there was also a ruthless demand to his kiss, a fierce assault on both mind and body that held her stunned and unmoving. His mouth shifted over hers, subduing any hint of resistance, taking with a relentless thirst, but also giving a wealth of passion in return. One hand settled low on her back, arching her into the tight cradle of his thighs. His other hand slid up her spine, beneath the heavy fall of her braid, his fingers thrusting through the silken strands of her hair and cupping her head.

Unable to help herself, she felt her arms tighten around him, discovering again the breadth of his shoulders and the lean, compact muscles sculpting his ribs and chest. With trembling fingers she searched out the tiny mole that hid in the hollow at the base of his throat, knowing that she should fight him, that she should end this farce. But somehow she couldn't. He'd been her first lover... her only lover. There was a connection between them that could never be severed, much as she might wish it otherwise.

He deepened the kiss between them, his thumb sliding along her jaw to the corner of her mouth and teasing the sensitive spot until her lips parted beneath his. To her shame, she kissed him back, kissed him with eight lonely years' worth of pent-up yearning. She needed this moment out of time, and part of her rejoiced in the exquisite memories his touch resurrected. She came alive in his arms, became the woman she'd once been. But another part of her, the part that had suffered at his hands, knew the danger, knew the price she'd pay for allowing him to sweep away the barriers she'd fought so hard to build. She couldn't afford to feel again. She'd almost been destroyed once by this man; she wouldn't offer him the opportunity to complete the job.

He kissed her at length, the conqueror staking his claim, and a small growl of satisfaction rumbled deep in his chest. It was that tiny sound which finally brought her to her senses. She fought her way free of his embrace and retreated several steps across the porch. Raising trembling fingers to her mouth, she stared at him...stared in stunned disbelief at Hunter Pryde—the one man she'd hoped never to see again.

He returned her look, his expression one of cool amusement. 'Hello, Leah,' he said. 'It's been a long time.'

His careless words brought a world of hurt. She struggled to conceal her devastation, to hide the pain his kiss had resurrected. After all that had gone before, after all they had once meant to each other, how could he be so casual, so heartless? Hadn't he caused enough anguish by walking out on her without...this?

'It hasn't been long enough, as far as I'm concerned. Why are you here, Hunter?' she demanded in a raw voice. 'What do you want?'

He smiled briefly, a flash of white teeth in a bronzed face. 'You know what I want. The same thing I've always wanted.'

She shook her head in desperation. 'No. Not the ranch.'

'The ranch? Try again, Leah.' He reached into his shirt pocket and retrieved a newspaper clipping. 'I've come in response to your ad.'

A small gasp escaped. 'You can't be serious,' she protested.

'I'm very serious.'

His voice held an implicit warning and she took another unthinking step away from him. 'You...you can't do this. You don't even have an appointment!' She used the first ridiculous excuse that occurred to her, but she was grasping at straws and they both knew it.

'Would you have given me one?' he asked, seemingly content to play the game her way. For now.

'Not a chance.'

'No. I didn't think so. Which is why I answered your ad under the name H.P. Smith.'

Briefly, she shut her eyes. After her experience with Titus T. Culpepper, she'd pinned ridiculously high hopes on the unknown H.P. Smith. So much for dreaming of a knight in shining armor. Hunter Pryde was no knight—a former lover, a one-time wrangler on her father's ranch, and a thief who'd stolen her heart before vanishing like the morning mist—but no knight. More likely he'd prove to be one more battle she'd have to fight...and win.

He tucked her ad back into his shirt pocket and cupped her elbow. 'Inside, Leah. We have a lot to discuss.'

'No!' she protested, yanking free of his grasp. 'I have nothing to discuss with you.'

He bent down, picked up her rifle and emptied the chamber of shells. He stared first at the slugs in his hand, then at her. 'I suggest you reconsider,' he told her.

It took every ounce of self-possession not to apologize for shooting at him. She faced him, hands planted on her hips. 'You're not wanted here.' She gestured toward the rifle, adding drily, 'You should have taken the hint.'

'Last chance, Leah. You don't want to fight me on this.'

The words were arctic-cold, the threat inexorable. He gazed down at her, and the expression in his eyes almost stopped her breath. Why did he look at her like that—

as though all the sins in the world could be laid at her doorstep and he'd come to exact retribution? She'd done nothing to him, except love him. And he'd repaid that love with desertion. His fierce gaze continued to hold her, and with a sudden, gut-wrenching certainty she realized that somehow she'd wronged him and he'd come to even the score. She fought a mind-numbing panic. If she succumbed to panic she didn't stand a chance against him.

Instinct urged her to throw him off her property and be done with it. But she didn't have that luxury. Knowing him, he wouldn't go until he'd had his say. Instead, she'd handle this in a calm, intelligent manner. She'd hear him out—not that she had much choice in the matter. Then she'd throw him off her property.

'Leah,' Hunter prompted in a surprisingly gentle voice.

She didn't allow his mildness to mislead her. The softer he spoke, the more dangerous he became. Right now, he was deadly serious. 'All right, Hunter.' She forced out the words. 'We'll play it your way... for the time being.'

He rattled the rifle-slugs fisted in his hand, the sound more sinister than any made by a diamond-back snake. Settling his hat more firmly on his head, he snagged her elbow, his grip firm and purposeful. 'Let's go.'

She didn't flinch. Instead, she allowed herself to be drawn into the house. Peeking up at his rigid features, she released a silent sigh. With no rescue in sight, it looked as if she'd fight this battle alone. And she could, too.

So long as he didn't touch her again.

Once inside the study, Hunter closed the door and crossed to the far wall, where the family photos hung. He paused, assessing them, one in particular seeming to capture his attention. It had been taken around the time he'd known her; she'd been just eighteen.

In the picture she sat on a fence-rail, faded jeans clinging to her coltish legs, a sleeveless checked shirt revealing slim, sun-browned arms. She stared off into the distance, a half-smile curving her mouth, her gaze unfocused as though her thoughts were far, far away. Just as the picture had been snapped she'd raised a hand to her cheek, brushing a stray curl from her face.

'I expected your hair to have darkened.' He glanced from the photo to Leah. 'It hasn't. It's still almost silver. As I recall, it used to flow through my fingers like silk. I wonder if it still would.'

'Stop it, Hunter,' she ordered tightly.

He glanced back at the photo. 'It doesn't do you justice, you know.'

'What, the picture?' She shrugged uneasily. 'If you say so. I think it looks just like I used to.'

'Not quite.' His mouth curled to one side. 'It doesn't show the passion . . . nor the ruthlessness. Even at that age you had a surplus of both.' He turned to study her. 'Do you still?'

Her mouth tightened. 'I've changed a lot since then. You figure out how.'

Turning away, she took a stance behind the huge oak desk, hoping it would put her in a stronger, more authoritative position. She hoped in vain. Hunter removed his hat, dropped it in the middle of the desk and edged his hip on to the corner nearest her.

'You knew the ad in the paper was mine, didn't you?' she began, determined to get their confrontation over as quickly as possible. 'How?'

'The nickname you used. Miss Bluebonnet.'

She nodded in acknowledgement. 'Dad used to call me that because of my eyes.' Then, with a sigh, she asked,

'Why are you really here, Hunter? Because I don't believe for one minute that it's in response to that ad.'

'You know why I'm here,' he said.

'I can guess.' Pierced by eyes that were panther-black and jungle-watchful, she'd never felt so intimidated in her life. And it took every ounce of resolve not to let it show.

Hunter Pryde had changed, attained a sophistication she'd never have believed possible. Eight years ago he'd been in his mid-twenties and wild, both in appearance and in attitude. In those days his black hair had brushed his shoulders, held back by a leather thong, his eyes reflecting a savage determination to succeed in a world just as determined to see him fail. But what had attracted her most had been his face—the high, sculpted cheekbones, the hawk-like nose, and the tough, bronzed features that reflected an unmistakable strength and vitality.

His long-limbed arms and legs, his broad chest and lean, sinewy build spoke of a mix of conquistadors and native American Indian, of a proud and noble heritage. When he'd taken her into his arms she'd sensed that no one else would ever make her come alive the way she did with him, that she'd never love anyone quite as much.

And she'd been right.

'You've come to see the Hamptons broken, is that it?' Leah asked with a directness she knew he'd appreciate.

A cynical smile touched his mouth. 'Swayed, never broken. Wasn't that your father's motto? No. I've come to discover why, if things are so bad, you haven't sold out. Are you really so destitute that you need to resort to this?' Removing the ad once more from his shirt pocket, he balled it in his fist and flicked the crumpled newspaper toward the trash can. It arched over the rim and hit the bottom with a faint metallic thud.

He couldn't have made his disapproval any clearer. She found it mortifying that he, of all people, had happened across that ad. But she wasn't a shy, easily coerced teenager any more. And she wouldn't be bullied. Not by anyone. Certainly not by Hunter.

'This isn't any of your business,' she informed him. 'I don't owe you a thing, least of all an explanation for my actions.'

'I'm making it my business,' he corrected in a hard, resolute voice. 'And, one way or another, I will have an explanation.'

She struggled to curb her anger. It wasn't easy. He had an uncanny knack for driving her into an uncontrollable fury. 'Are you really interested,' she snapped, 'or have you come to gloat?'

He folded his arms across his chest. 'I wouldn't be here if I wasn't interested.'

'Fine.' She'd try taking him at his word and see where it led. Though she suspected she wouldn't like it when they got there. 'I didn't have any choice but to place that ad.'

He dismissed her excuse with a contemptuous gesture. 'Don't give me that. We always have choices. You just have a knack for picking the wrong ones.'

'You may not agree with my decisions, but that doesn't make them wrong,' she retorted, stung. 'The last few years haven't been easy. Dad...Dad died a year after you left.' Hunter's leaving at a time she needed him most still hurt, even after all these years. Until he'd ridden up today, she hadn't realized how much of that pain lingered.

'Yes, I know.'

She flinched. 'You knew?' Knew and never bothered to return? Never bothered to see how she was, see if she required any help or support? She straightened her shoulders. No, not support. She'd support herself. And her grandmother. And the ranch. And all those she'd gathered beneath her wing. No matter what it cost.

'I read his obit in the papers.' He leaned closer, and she caught her breath, drawing in the rich, spicy scent of his aftershave. 'I understand the ranch has gone downhill ever since. You may be just as ruthless and single-minded as your old man, but you're sure as hell not the rancher he was.'

She jerked as though slapped, and for a moment the defiant, protective mask she'd kept rigidly in place slipped, leaving her vulnerable and exposed. How could she ever have been seduced by this man? Even at eighteen she should have had the sense to see the cold, heartless soul that ruled his keen intellect, no matter how attractive the outer packing.

'I won't defend myself to you. Why should I? Nor will I be judged by your yardstick,' she insisted fiercely. 'So spit out what you came to say and get the hell off my land.'

She saw the familiar spark of anger flicker to life in his eyes and wondered if she'd pushed him too far. Not that she cared. With her back against the wall, both literally and figuratively, she'd fight free any way she could and damn the consequences.

With an abrupt sweep of his arm he snagged her waist, and forced her between his legs. 'Don't you know why I'm here?' He cupped her shoulders to curb her instinctive opposition, rough amusement edging his words.

As much as she wanted to tell him to go to hell, she knew he wouldn't release her until she'd answered. Glaring at him, she said, 'You came in response to the ad.'

'More than that, Leah. Much, much more,' he corrected, a bitter smile twisting his mouth. 'I came for the ranch.' His eyes grew black and pitiless, searing her with a burning determination. 'And ... I came for you.'

CHAPTER TWO

SHOCK held Leah immobile for a split-second. Recovering swiftly, she lifted her chin. 'That's a real shame, Hunter,' she retorted, continuing to fight his hold. 'Because you aren't getting either one.'

His grip tightened. 'We'll see.'

She stopped struggling. Resistance was fruitless. Instead, she used the only other weapon she possessed. Words. 'Did you really believe that after all these years you could just come strolling back up my drive? Your arrogance is incredible. After what you did to me, I wouldn't give you so much as the time of day!'

'A little melodramatic, don't you think?'

Fury ripped through her and she gave in to it, needing the satisfaction losing her temper would provide. 'Melodramatic? Not by a long shot. You stole my innocence, you bastard. And you did it solely to get your hands on this ranch.' Bitterness spilled over, pouring out after years of suppression. Her pain, her agony, stripped of any protective cover, lay bare for him to see. 'I was eighteen and crazy in love. And you used me. *You used me!*'

'The hell I did. I just took what you offered.'

His cruelty cut her to the quick and it required all her willpower not to hit him. But she remembered his lightning-fast speed of old. Her blow would never land and his retaliation would be swift and unpleasant. She looked him straight in the eye. 'You can't get out of your responsibilities that easily. You took exactly what you wanted, no matter who suffered in the process.'

His mouth settled into a grim line. 'You never knew what I wanted. You still don't.'

'Oh, no?' Did he really consider her so blind, so ignorant of man's baser motivations? Perhaps eight years ago she'd been guilty of such an oversight, but no longer. He'd cured her of that. 'It's the same then as now. You want my land. Well, get in line.'

'There is no line,' he bit out. 'Nor will there be. You'd better face that fact right here and now.'

He tugged her closer, as though to obstruct any chance of flight. Slowly, relentlessly, he gathered her in, trapping her in a grasp as binding and inescapable as a mist-net around a struggling sparrow. She pressed her hands against his chest, striving to keep some small distance between them. But instead she found that touching him only resurrected long-forgotten emotions, reminding her of all that had gone before. Tears threatened, but she ruthlessly forced them back. Tears wouldn't accomplish a thing. Not with this man.

'Why are you doing this?' she asked. 'Why now, after all this time?'

'Because it will give me what I want most.'

She laughed quietly, the sound one of pain and disillusionment rather than amusement. 'When you said that eight years ago, I foolishly thought you meant me. But now I realize you meant the ranch.'

His expression closed over. 'Did I?'

'Yes! Is that why you bedded me? Because it would give you your dream? It didn't work out that way, did it?'

'Bedded you? A rather quaint description for what we did together. Something a bit more elemental and a lot cruder would be closer to the truth. And, as I recall, we never did get around to using a bed.'

She refused to feel shame for an act that had been the most beautiful experience of her life. 'No, we didn't. Because you left before we ever had the chance. Of course, you didn't hit the road until Dad threatened to disinherit me. He offered me a choice. You or the ranch.'

'And we both know which you chose.'

She caught his shirt in her fists. 'How would you know that?' she demanded passionately, her distress breaking free of her control. 'You didn't stick around long enough to find out. But I can guarantee choosing you was a mistake I've lived to regret. It never occurred to me that, without the ranch, I wasn't much of a bargain.' Her pride had suffered from that knowledge. But her pride had handled the battering. Her heart hadn't been nearly so sturdy. 'So you took what you could and walked.'

A hard smile tilted his mouth to one side and his hands closed over hers, prying them free of his shirt. 'Let's be accurate. I didn't walk. I was dragged.'

'Don't give me that. I waited in the line-shack for hours. Does that amuse you?' Her breathing grew shallow and rapid, the dark recollections ones she rarely dredged from her memory. 'The afternoon was sweltering, but I waited inside the cabin for you anyway. I was so afraid one of the wranglers would stop by... that there'd be some unexpected strays to round up or fence to string and he'd decide to spend the night out there and I'd get caught. But I didn't leave. I kept telling myself you'd come. The hours became an eternity, as though the world had moved on and I'd somehow been left behind. Even after the sun set, I found excuse after excuse to explain your absence.'

'Stop it, Leah.'

But she couldn't. Once started, the memories continued to unravel, like a wind-up music-box grinding out its song until the music played down. 'It was a full moon that night. I sat on the floor and watched as it drifted from window to window, inching a path across the sky.'

He stared at her, impassive and remote. 'It rained.'

Surfacing from the remembered nightmare, she focused on his face. 'Not until two that morning,' she corrected, her voice dull and lifeless. 'The storm rolled in from the south and blotted out the stars as though an angry hand had wiped them from the sky. The roof leaked like a sieve but, fool that I was, I stayed.' She bowed her head, her emotions nearly spent. 'I stayed and stayed and stayed.'

'Why? Why did you stay?' he asked insistently. 'Look at me, Leah. Look me in the eye and tell me the rest of your lies. Because that's all they are.'

'How could you possibly know what's fact and what's fiction,' she whispered, 'when you weren't there to see?'

'Tell me!'

Forced by the relentless command, she lifted her head. He swept a wisp of ash-blonde hair from her face, and though he touched her with a tender hand his expression was anything but.

'I stayed because I was waiting for you to ride up and take me away like you promised,' she admitted, her voice breaking. 'At daybreak I finally realized you weren't coming. And I vowed that I'd never trust a man again. I'd never give him that sort of power over me or leave myself open and vulnerable to that much misery. So tell me, Hunter. Tell me the truth. What happened? What was so vital that it *dragged* you away and you couldn't be bothered to come back?'

'Sheriff Lomax happened.'

It took a long minute for his words to sink in. 'What do you mean?' she asked, dread balling in her stomach.

He laughed, the jarring sound slicing across her nerves like a finely honed blade. 'Cut the bull, Leah. All that nonsense about waiting for me at the line-shack and sweltering in the heat and watching the moon. It didn't happen. I know it. And you know it. Though I did enjoy the part about the roof leaking. Very pathetic.'

'What's the sheriff got to do with this?' she demanded, more urgently.

'I went to the line-shack, as agreed. You weren't there.' He paused significantly. 'The sheriff was. Along with a few of his men.'

'No. I don't believe you.'

'It took six of them to pull me out of there. You forgot to mention, in your heartbreaking tale of woe, about the smashed furniture or the broken window. Or the unhinged door. They might have taken me, but I didn't go easy.'

'I don't know...' She struggled to remember. Had the window and furniture been broken? 'Things were a bit of a mess, but——'

He didn't give her a chance to finish. 'I guess you were so busy staring at the stars you didn't notice.' Catching hold of her long, silver braid, he wound it around his hand, pulling her close. His mouth hovered a hair's-breadth above hers. 'Or maybe you didn't notice because every word you've uttered is a lie. Admit it. You were never at that line-shack.'

'I was there!'

'Not a chance. Only two people knew about our meeting. You... and me. I didn't tell a soul. But, since the sheriff came in your place, there's only one explanation. You changed your mind. And, afraid of how I'd react, you spilled your guts to Daddy and begged him to get you out of a sticky situation.'

'No! It didn't happen that way.'

'Didn't it? Tell me this. If we had met that afternoon, would you have come away with me? Well...?' He pinned her with a hard, savage gaze. 'Would you?'

She'd never lied to him in the past and she wouldn't start now. No matter how it might look to him, no matter how he might react, she'd tell him the truth. 'No. I wouldn't have gone with you.'

For an instant his grip tightened and she waited for him to master his anger, unafraid, knowing with an absolute certainty that he'd never physically harm her. 'I didn't think so,' he said. He released her and stood, and she sensed that he'd set himself apart, distancing himself from her.

Her explanation wouldn't change anything, but she had to try. For the first time she deliberately touched him, placing a hand on his upper arm, feeling the rock-like muscles clench in reaction. 'There's a reason I wouldn't have gone away with you——'

'Enough, Leah.' He turned flat, cold eyes in her direction. 'I've heard enough. It's water under the bridge. And, to be honest, your excuses don't interest me.'

There was no point in trying to force him to listen. Not now. Maybe not ever. 'Then why are you here?' she asked. 'Why cause more grief—grief neither of us needs?'

'Because what's important is today. Here and now. Your ranch and that ad.'

'I won't let you get your hands on this ranch...or on me,' she informed him fiercely. 'You might as well give up and move on, because I won't marry you.'

He laughed, the sound harsh and mocking. 'I don't recall asking, sweetheart.'

A tide of color washed into her face at his biting response. 'I assumed that was why you'd come. You had the ad and you implied——'

He lifted an eyebrow. 'Implied what?'

'That you were interested in marrying me,' she maintained stubbornly. 'You came in response to my notice, didn't you?'

'Not to offer marriage, that's for damned sure. I came because you wouldn't have placed that ad if you weren't desperate, which makes it a powerful bargaining chip. So let's bargain. I want the ranch, Leah, and I mean to get it.'

They stared at each other for an endless moment. Before she could respond, a car horn sounded out front, and Hunter glanced towards the windows. 'Someone's here. Another applicant, perhaps?'

Slipping past him, Leah crossed to the window, recognizing the pick-up parked in front. The occupant leaned on the horn again and her mouth tightened in response. 'It would appear this is my day for surprises,' she murmured. 'Unpleasant surprises, that is.' She crossed to the picture wall where Hunter had left her rifle and snatched it up.

'What's going on, Leah?' Hunter demanded, picking up his hat. 'Who's your company?'

Intent on reloading, she spared him a brief glance. 'His name is Bull Jones. He's the foreman of the Circle P.'

Hunter's eyes narrowed. 'The Circle P?'

'A new outfit. Actually, they're now the *only* outfit in these parts, except for us. They're owned by a big conglomerate, Lyon Enterprises, and they're not particularly friendly. So do me a favor and stay out of this, okay? It doesn't concern you.'

He looked as if he might debate the issue. Then, with an abrupt nod, he followed her out to the porch. Propping his shoulder against a pillar, he tipped his hat low on his brow, his face thrown into shadow. Satisfied by Hunter's apparent compliance, Leah turned her attention to the more immediate and far more menacing problem confronting her.

Bull Jones leaned negligently against the door of his pick-up—a pick-up parked directly in the middle of the tiny strip of flowerbed Grandmother Rose had painstakingly labored over these past three weeks. 'Afternoon, Miz Hampton,' he said, grinning around the stub of a thick cigar.

She ignored his greeting, taking a stand at the top of the porch steps. 'Get off my property, you thieving rattlesnake,' she ordered coldly, 'before I call the sheriff.'

'In one of your feisty moods, are you?' She didn't bother responding and he sighed. 'Call the sheriff if it'll make you feel any better. But you know and I know he won't be coming. He's tired of all your phone-calls.'

She couldn't argue with the truth. Instead, she brought the rifle to her shoulder and aimed the hurting end exactly six inches below Bull's massive silver belt buckle. 'Spit out why you came and get the hell off my land before I send you home with a few vital parts missing,' she said.

He didn't seem the least intimidated. In fact he laughed in genuine amusement. 'You do have a way with words.' He jerked his head toward Hunter. 'This *hombre* one of your prospective suitors? Doesn't have much to say for himself.'

Hunter smiled without amusement. 'Give it time, friend.'

Leah couldn't conceal her surprise. If Bull considered Hunter a potential suitor, then he knew about her advertisement. But how had he found out? Before the two men could exchange further words, she hastened to ask, 'Is that it, Jones? That's what you came about? My ad?'

'One of the reasons,' Bull acknowledged. 'I even considered offering myself up as a possible candidate. But I didn't think you'd go for it.'

'You thought right.'

'As to the other matter....' He paused to savor his cigar, puffing contentedly for a long minute. She knew it was a deliberate maneuver on his part—an attempt to drive her crazy. Unfortunately it was working.

'Out with it, Jones.'

'My, my. You are in a hurry.' He shrugged, a quick grin sliding across his face. 'You want it straight? Okay. I'll give it to you straight. I came to offer a friendly little warning.'

'*Friendly*?'

'I'm a friendly sort of guy.' He took a step in her direction. 'You give me half the chance, you'd find just how friendly I can be.'

She didn't know whether it was the sound of her pumping home the shell in her rifle or the fact that Hunter suddenly straightened from his lounging position that stopped Bull in his tracks. Whichever it was, he froze. Then she glanced at Hunter and knew what had checked the foreman's movements.

She'd always found Hunter's eyes fascinating. One minute the blackness appeared, cold and remote, the next minute glittering with fire and passion. For the first time she saw his eyes burn with an implacable threat and for the first time she realized how intimidating it could be.

He leveled that look on Bull. 'If you have something more to say,' he informed the foreman softly, 'I suggest you say it. Fast.'

Bull Jones shot Hunter a look of fury, but Leah noticed he obeyed. 'Seems Lyon Enterprises is getting tired of playing games over this place.' His gaze shifted to Leah. 'Thought you should know they've decided to call in the big guns.'

'I'm shaking in my boots,' she said.

He removed his cigar from between his teeth and threw it to the ground. It landed amongst a clump of crushed pink begonias, wisps of smoke drifting up from the smoldering tip. 'You will be. From what I hear, this new guy's tough. You don't stand a chance.'

His words terrified her. But she refused to crack. She wouldn't allow her fear to show. Not to this bastard. 'You've been saying that for a full year now,' she said calmly enough. 'And I've managed just fine.'

'That was kid-glove treatment.'

Anger stirred. The temptation to pull the trigger and be done with it was all too inviting. 'You call fouling wells and cutting fence-line and stampeding my herd kid-glove treatment?'

He shrugged. 'We were having a little fun, is all. But now the gloves are off. Don't say I didn't warn you.'

With that, he stomped through what remained of Grandmother Rose's flowerbed and climbed into his pick-up. The engine started with a noisy roar and he gunned it, a rooster-tail of dirt and grass spraying up from beneath his rear wheels. They watched in silence as he disappeared down the dirt drive. A minute later all that remained of Bull's passing was a tiny whirlwind of dust, spinning lazily in the distance. Leah eyed it with a thoughtful frown.

Hunter slipped the rifle from her grasp and leaned it against the porch rail. 'Something you forgot to tell me?' he murmured sardonically.

She lifted her chin. 'There might be one or two minor details we didn't get around to discussing. Not that it's any concern of yours.'

'I don't agree. I suggest we go back inside and discuss those minor details.'

'No!' She rounded on him. First Titus T., then Bull and now Hunter. This definitely wasn't her day. 'You know full well that there's nothing left to talk over. You want the ranch and I won't let you have it. Even if you were interested in responding to my ad—interested in marriage—I won't choose you for the position. How could you think I would?'

He raised an eyebrow. 'Position? I thought you wanted a husband.'

'That's right, I do. But since you aren't interested...' Fighting to keep the distress from her voice, she said, 'You've had your fun. So why don't you leave?'

He shook his head. 'We're not through with our conversation, and I'm not leaving until we are. If that means applying for your...position, then consider me applied.'

'Forget it. You don't qualify,' she insisted. 'That ends the conversation as far as I'm concerned.'

'I qualify, all right. On every point.'

She didn't want to continue with this charade but, aside from picking up her rifle and trying to force him off her property at gunpoint, she didn't see any other option available to her. Especially considering how far she'd gotten the last time she'd turned her rifle on him. 'Fine. You think you qualify? Then prove it,' she demanded.

'A challenge? Not a wise move, Leah, because once I've proven myself we'll finish that discussion.' He tilted his head to one side, his brow furrowed in thought. 'Let's see if I can get this right... Number one. You want a man between the ages of twenty-five and forty-five. No problem there.'

'You should have read the ad more carefully, Hunter! It says a *kind and gentle* man. You are neither kind nor gentle.'

His gaze, black and merciless, met hers. 'You'd do well to remember that.'

Tempted as she was, she didn't back down. 'I haven't forgotten. The ad also says applicants should be looking for a permanent type of relationship.' She shot him a skeptical glance. 'Don't tell me you're finally ready to settle down?'

'That isn't my first choice, no. But I'd consider it if the right offer came along. Number two. As I recall that concerns ranching experience.' He folded his arms across his chest. 'You planning to debate my qualifications there?'

She shook her head. After all, there was nothing to debate. 'I'll concede your ranching abilities,' she agreed.

A grim smile touched his mouth. 'You'll concede a hell of a lot more before we're finished. Number three. He should also have solid business skills—particularly those skills necessary to please a bullheaded banker.' He settled his hat lower on his forehead. 'You've tipped your hand with that one.'

'Have I?' Something about his attitude worried her. He acted as though this were all a game, as though she'd already lost the match but didn't yet know it. What she couldn't figure was...how? How could she lose a game that she wasn't even playing?

His smile turned predatory. 'You're having financial difficulties and the bank won't help without a man backing you. Close enough?'

She gritted her teeth. 'Close enough,' she forced herself to confess. 'But you aren't that man. End of discussion.'

'Far from it. There isn't a bank in the world who wouldn't back me.'

That gave her pause. 'Since when?'

He closed the distance between them, crowding her against the porch rail. 'It's been eight years since our last meeting. A lot has happened in that time. I'm not the poor ranch-hand you once knew. You need me, Leah. And soon—very soon—I'm going to prove it to you.'

'I don't need you!' she denied passionately. 'I'll *never* need you.'

'Yes, you will.' His voice dropped, the timbre soft and caressing, but his words were as hard and chipped as stone. 'Because you won't get any cooperation from the bank without me. I guarantee it. And by tomorrow you'll know it, too.'

She caught her breath. 'You can prove that?'

'I'll give you all the proof you need. Count on it.' He lowered his head, his mouth inches from hers. 'Seems I've qualified after all.'

She glared, slipping from between him and the rail. 'I disagree. You've already admitted that you aren't kind or gentle. And since that *is* one of the qualifications...' She shrugged. ''Fraid I'll have to pass.'

'And I'm afraid I'll have to insist. In the business world all negotiations are subject to compromise. You'll have to compromise on "kind and gentle".'

'And what will you compromise about?' she shot back.

'If I can get away with it...nothing.' He edged his hip on to the rail and glanced at her. 'Tell me something, Leah. Why haven't you sold the ranch?'

She shifted impatiently. 'I think you can guess. Hampton Homestead has been in our family for——'

'Generations. Yes, your father made that point quite clear. Along with the point that he wouldn't allow his ranch or his daughter to fall into the hands of some penniless mongrel whose bloodlines couldn't be traced past the orphanage where he'd been dumped.'

She stared at him, genuinely shocked. 'He said that to you?'

'He said it. But that's not the point. You're out of options, Leah. Soon you won't have any other alternative. My sources tell me that either you sell or you go bankrupt. At least if you sell you'll walk away with enough money to live in comfort.'

She lifted her chin. 'There is another alternative.'

His mouth twisted. 'The ad.'

'Don't look at me like that! It's not as foolish a decision as you might think. The banks will loan me the money I need to stay afloat if I have a husband who's both a businessman and a rancher.'

He stilled. 'They've guaranteed you the money?'

She shook her head. 'Not in writing, if that's what you mean. But Conrad Michaels is the senior loan officer and an old family friend. And, though he hasn't been in a position to help us in the past, he feels our business reversals are correctable, with some work. He's a bit... old-fashioned. It was his idea that I find an appropriate husband. He hasn't been able to get the loan committee to approve financing so far, but he's positive he can if I marry.'

She'd never seen Hunter look so furious. 'Are you telling me that this Michaels instructed you to advertise in the paper for a husband and you went along with his hare-brained notion?'

'It's not a hare-brained notion,' she protested. 'It's very practical. Conrad simply suggested I find a husband with the necessary qualifications as quickly as possible. Once I'd done that, he'd get the loan package put through.'

'He suggested that, did he? In his position as your banker?' Hunter didn't bother to conceal his contempt. 'Did it ever occur to you he could have trouble living

up to that promise? He has a board of directors to answer
to who might not agree with him any more now than
before. And then where would you be? Bankrupt and
married to some cowpoke who'll take whatever he can
lay hands on and toss you over when the going gets
tough.'

'You should know,' she shot back. 'You're a past
master of that fine art.'

'Don't start something you can't finish, Leah,' he
warned softly. 'I'm telling you—marry the next man who
responds to your ad and you'll sacrifice everything and
receive nothing but trouble.'

'You're wrong,' she said with absolute confidence. 'I
have faith in Conrad. He'll put the loan through.'

She could tell Hunter didn't agree, but he kept his
opinion to himself. 'What about the ad?' he asked.

'The ad was my idea. I needed results and I needed
them fast.' She folded her arms across her chest in perfect
imitation of his stance. 'And I got them.'

He laughed without amusement. 'If you got "kind
and gentle" I'm less than impressed.'

'It's not you who has to be impressed,' she retorted
defensively. 'It's Conrad whose approval I need.'

'I don't doubt your banker friend will make sure your
prospective husband is qualified as a rancher and a
businessman,' he stated with marked disapproval. 'But
what about as a husband and lover? Who's going to
make sure he qualifies in that area?' Hunter's voice
dropped, the sound rough and seductive. '"Kind and
gentle" couldn't satisfy you in bed in a million years.'

She silently cursed the color surging into her cheeks.
'That's the least of my concerns.'

'You're right. It will be.' He regarded her with de-
rision. 'Is that how you see married life? A sterile part-

nership with a husband who hasn't a clue how to please
his wife?'

Images leapt to her mind, images of the two of them
entwined beneath an endless blue sky, their clothes scattered haphazardly around them, their nudity cloaked by
thick, knee-high grass. She resisted the seductive pull of
the memory. She couldn't afford to remember those
times, couldn't afford to risk her emotions on something so fleeting and uncertain...nor so painful. Not if
she intended to save the ranch.

'That's not important,' she stated coldly. 'Conrad has
promised that if I marry someone the bank considers a
sound businessman and rancher, I'll get my loan. And
that's what I intend to do. Period. End of discussion.
I'm keeping this ranch even if it means accepting the
first qualified man who walks through my door. And
nothing you say or do will change that.'

'I've got news for you. I *am* the first qualified man
to walk through your door. The first and the last.' He
reached into his pocket and retrieved a business card.
'Perhaps you'd better know who you're up against.'

'No, let me tell you who *you're* up against,' she retorted, almost at the end of her rope. 'That huge
company I mentioned—Lyon Enterprises—is after this
ranch. And they'll use any means necessary to acquire
it. You've met Bull Jones. He's encouraged almost all
my workers to leave with exorbitant bribes. Nor was I
kidding when I accused him of cutting my fences and
stampeding my herd and fouling the wells. The man I
marry will have to contend with that.' She planted her
hands on her hips. 'Well, Hunter? Maybe now that you
have all the facts in your possession you'll decide to get
out of my life. Just be sure that when you do, you make
it for good.'

His eyes narrowed and, in a move so swift she didn't see it coming, he caught her by the elbows and swung her into his arms. She slammed into him, the breath knocked from her lungs. 'Don't threaten me, Leah. You won't like the results,' he warned curtly. 'Give it to me straight. Are you really being harassed, or is this another of your imaginative little fantasies?'

This time she didn't even try to fight his hold. She'd learned the hard way how pointless it would be. 'It's no fantasy! You saw a prime example today. Or ask my foreman. Patrick will tell you. He's one of the few they haven't managed to run off.'

His eyes glittered with barely suppressed wrath and a frown slashed deep furrows across his brow. Without releasing her, he tucked his business card back into his pocket. 'You're serious, aren't you?'

She nodded. 'Dead serious.'

'You're also serious about marrying, even if it means losing the ranch?'

'I am.'

'In that case you're down to one option.'

She sighed, weary of their argument. 'I told you. I'm not selling.'

'No, you're not. You're going to marry me.'

If he hadn't been holding her, she would have fallen. 'What?' she whispered, unable to hide her shock.

'You heard me. We'll marry and I'll see to it that you get your loan.'

She stared at him in bewilderment, the fierce determination she read there filling her with a sense of unease. 'You said... I thought you didn't want to marry me.'

'It wasn't my first choice, no,' he agreed. 'But the more I consider the idea, the greater the appeal.'

She caught her breath. 'That's the most insulting offer I've ever heard.'

'Count on it,' he said with a grim smile. 'I can get much more insulting than that.'

'I wouldn't advise it,' she snapped back. 'Not if you'd like me to accept.'

He inclined his head, but whether in acknowledgement or concurrence she wasn't quite clear. An endless moment stretched between them, a moment where they fought a silent battle of wills. It wasn't an even match. Slowly, Leah lowered her eyes. 'You agree,' Hunter stated in satisfaction.

'I didn't say that.' She stalled for time—not that it would help. Exhaustion dogged her heels, making it impossible to think straight. She needed time alone, time to consider, time to put all he'd told her into perspective. But she strongly suspected she wouldn't be given that time. 'What about the bank? Can you guarantee I'll get the loan?'

His expression hardened. 'I have some small influence. I'm not the poor, mixed-breed cur I was eight years ago.'

'I never saw you that way,' she reacted instantly, despising the crude comparison. 'And if my father did, he was wrong.'

He shrugged off her rejoinder. 'What's your decision, Leah?'

This time she did try and free herself. Not that she succeeded. 'What's your rush?' she asked. His touch grew gentle, soothing rather than restraining, at striking odds with his clipped tone. Had he decided an illusion of tenderness might better influence her? If so, he'd soon discover his mistake.

'I don't want anyone else coming along messing up my deal. You have twenty-four hours to make up your mind. Sell the ranch to me or marry me; I don't give a damn which. Because I know it all, Leah,' he informed her tautly. 'I've had your financial situation investigated. You're broke. Without a loan you'll go bankrupt. And without me you won't get that loan.'

She caught her breath in disbelief. 'I don't believe you!'

'You will. You will when the banks tell you that I'm your only choice other than bankruptcy.'

She shook her head, desperate to deny his words. 'How can you possibly do that?'

'You'd be surprised at what I can do.'

'What's happened to you?' she whispered. 'Mercy used to be a part of your nature.'

He gazed at her impassively. 'Not any more. You saw to that. It's your decision. And to help you decide...'

She knew what he intended; she recognized the passion in his expression, saw the resolve in his eyes. To her eternal disgust she lifted her face to meet his kiss. Curiosity, that was all it was, she told herself. But she lied. Her curiosity had been appeased earlier. She knew from that first kiss that her reaction to his touch hadn't changed, not even after eight years.

No, she returned his kiss because she wanted to experience the wonder of it again. To come alive beneath his mouth and hands. To relive, if only for a moment, the mind-splintering rapture only he could arouse. He took his time, drinking his fill, sharing the passion that blazed with such incredible urgency.

But it was all an illusion. She knew that. He wanted the ranch and would use any means available to get it. Even seducing her. Even marrying her. And she'd be a fool to forget that.

Lifting his head, he gazed down at her. 'What we once had isn't finished, Leah,' he informed her in a rough, husky voice. 'There's still something between us. Something that needs to be settled, once and for all.'

She eased back. 'And you think our marriage will settle it?'

'One way or another,' he confirmed.

'You don't leave me much choice.'

'I've left you one choice. And I'm it.'

He set her from him, his expression once more cool and distant. In that instant she hated him. Hated him for making her want again. Hated him for resurrecting all that she'd struggled so hard to forget. But she especially hated him for being able to turn off his emotions with so little effort. Because she knew her emotions weren't as easily mastered.

'Twenty-four hours, Leah. After that, you're history.' And, without another word, he left her.

Long after he'd ridden away she stood on the front porch, unable to move, unable to think. Finally, with a muffled sob, she buried her head in her hands and allowed the tears to come.

CHAPTER THREE

HUNTER walked into his office and set his briefcase on his desk. A brief knock sounded on the door behind him and his assistant, Kevin Anderson, poked his head in the door.

'Oh, you're back. How did it go? Did she agree to sell the ranch?'

Opening his briefcase, Hunter removed a bulky file and tossed it to one side. 'Not yet. But I'll have it soon...one way or another.' He turned and faced his assistant, allowing his displeasure to show. 'Why didn't you tell me about Bull Jones and what he's been up to?'

'The foreman?' Kevin hesitated, then shrugged. 'I didn't think it was important.'

Anger made Hunter speak more sharply than he would have otherwise. 'Well, it damned well is important. You don't make those decisions. I do.'

'Sorry, boss. It won't happen again,' came Kevin's swift apology. Then he asked cautiously, 'I assume you've made the foreman's acquaintance?'

'In a manner of speaking.'

'Did he recognize you?'

Hunter didn't answer immediately. Instead, he crossed to the window and stared out at the Houston skyline. The intense humidity from the Gulf of Mexico rippled the air on the far side of the thick, tinted glass, signaling the start of another South Texas heatwave. 'No,' he finally said. 'He didn't recognize me. But then I didn't go out of my way to introduce myself.'

'That's probably smart. What do you want done about him?'

'Nothing for now.' Hunter turned back and faced his assistant. 'But I may need to take action in the future.'

'Whatever you say. You're the boss.'

Hunter inclined his head. 'One last thing before you go.'

'Sure. Anything.'

'You keep me informed from now on. No matter how minor or insignificant. I won't be caught off-guard again.'

'Yes, sir. Sorry, sir,' Kevin agreed. Then he quietly excused himself and slipped from the room.

After a brief hesitation Hunter crossed to his desk and flipped open the file marked 'Hampton Homestead.' A white tide of letters, legal documents and several photos spilled across the gleaming ebony surface. Reaching out, he selected two photos of Leah—one identical to the picture he'd studied in the Hampton study, the other a snapshot only a month old.

Examining the more recent of the two, a savage desire clawed through him, unexpected and intense. He still wanted her...wanted to rip her hair free of her braid, feel her silken limbs clinging to him, feel again her softness beneath him.

He dropped the photo to his desk. Soon, he promised himself. Very, very soon.

'We have to talk,' Grandmother Rose announced the next morning, slamming a thick porcelain mug in front of Leah.

Leah closed her eyes, stifling a groan. She hadn't slept a wink last night and could barely face the unrelenting morning sun, let alone a more unrelenting grandmother. 'If this is about Hunter, I don't want to discuss it.'

'It's about Hunter.'

'I don't want to discuss it.'

'Tough toenails. I have a confession to make and you're going to listen to every last word, even if I have to wrestle you to the floor and sit on you.'

The picture of her ninety-pound grandmother putting her in a headlock and forcing her to the tile floor brought a reluctant smile to Leah's mouth. 'Can we at least talk about the weather for five minutes while I drink my coffee?'

'It's sunny and eighty-five in the shade. Hope you swallowed fast. Now. About Hunter.'

Deep purplish-blue eyes held Leah's in a direct, steady gaze. The eye color and a relentless determination were only two of the qualities Leah shared with her grandmother. Unfortunately, Rose's determination included a stubbornness even beyond Leah's. She gave up. She'd never won an argument with her grandmother, a circumstance unlikely to change any time in the near future. 'What about him?' she asked with a sigh.

'What he said yesterday about the sheriff was true,' Rose announced. 'Every word.'

Leah straightened in her chair. 'You heard? You were listening?'

'I did and I was, and I'm not one bit ashamed to admit it. What I *am* ashamed to admit is that I betrayed your confidence to your father eight years ago.' She twisted her thick gold wedding-band around a knobby finger, the only external sign of her agitation.

'You warned Dad that I planned to run away with Hunter.' It wasn't a question. Leah had already figured out what must have happened. The only person she'd confessed to about that long-ago meeting sat across the table from her. Not that she'd ever expose her grandmother's involvement to Hunter.

'Yes, I told your father,' Rose confirmed. 'I told Ben because, selfishly, I didn't want you to leave.'

'But I promised you I wouldn't go!'

Leah shoved back her chair and stood. Struggling to conceal her distress, she made a production of pouring herself another cup of coffee. She'd told Rose about her meeting for one simple reason: she couldn't leave the woman who'd loved and raised her without a single word of farewell. What she hadn't anticipated was her grandmother's revelation that Leah's father was dying of cancer. Once in possession of the grim news she hadn't had any alternative. She couldn't abandon her father in his time of need, no matter how desperately she yearned to be with Hunter. It just wasn't in her nature.

Leah turned and faced her grandmother. 'I told you I'd meet Hunter and explain about Dad's illness. I planned to ask him to wait... to return after... after...'

Rose shrugged. 'Perhaps he'd have agreed. But I couldn't count on that—on his going away and letting you stay.' She sighed. 'Listen, girl, the reason I'm telling you all this is because I've decided. I want you to marry Hunter.'

Leah stared in shock. 'Come again?'

'What are you, deaf? I said, I want you to marry Hunter.'

'But... why?'

'Because...' Rose lifted her chin and confessed. 'Because I had a call from Conrad Michaels this morning.'

'What did he want?'

'Officially... to announce his retirement. Unofficially... to withdraw his offer of help. No bank loan in any circumstances was the message I got.'

'Hunter!' Leah released his name with a soft sigh.

'That thought occurred to me, too.' Her grandmother's eyes narrowed. 'You suppose his pull is strong enough to force Connie's retirement?'

'Possibly. Though if Hunter is as ruthless as you suspect, I'm surprised you're so anxious to marry me off to him.'

'Ruthless isn't bad...if it's working on your side. And, right now, we could use a whole lot of ruthless on our side.'

'Could we?' Leah questioned. 'I'm not so sure.'

Rose stared into her coffee-cup as though the answers to all their problems lay written in the dregs. Finally she glanced up, her expression as hard and set as Leah had ever seen it. 'You have two choices. You can sell or you can fight to win against Lyon Enterprises. If you want to sell, say the word, and we'll give up and clear out. But if you want to win, Hunter's the man for the job. It took you years to get over him. Fact is, I don't believe you ever did. Marry him or don't. It's your decision. But my vote is to snatch him up fast. Men like that only come along once in a lifetime. You've gotten a lucky break. He's come through your door twice.'

Lucky? Leah had her doubts. He'd loved her with a passion that she'd never forgotten and she'd let him down. He wouldn't give her the chance to hurt him like that again. She simply couldn't read too much into his return. If anything, he'd come back to wreak revenge. And, if that was the case, by placing that ad she had indeed exposed her vulnerability and given him the perfect opportunity to even an old score.

And he'd been swift to take advantage.

One by one he'd cut off every avenue of escape until she faced two tough alternatives. Unfortunately, learning that any possibility of a bank loan had been circumvented left her with no alternatives . . . if she intended to save the ranch.

Leah returned her mug to the counter, the coffee having gone stone-cold. She looked at her grandmother and saw the hint of desperation lurking in Rose's otherwise impassive expression. No matter what she'd said, losing the ranch would be the death of her. And to be responsible for her demise, when Leah had it within her power to prevent it, just couldn't be borne.

'I'll call Hunter,' she announced quietly.

For the first time in her life, Leah saw tears glitter in her grandmother's eyes. 'Don't accept his first offer, girl,' she advised gruffly. 'Bargain for position and you can still come out of this on top.'

'I'm not your granddaughter for nothing,' Leah said with a teasing smile. 'He won't have it all his own way.'

And he wouldn't. Very soon she'd find out just how badly he wanted the ranch—and just how much ground he'd give up in order to get it.

Not until Leah had completed her list of requests for Hunter—she hesitated to call them demands—did she realize that he hadn't left her a number where he could be reached. Not that it truly presented a problem. Precisely twenty-four hours after their original meeting, Hunter phoned.

'What's your answer?' he asked, dispensing with the preliminaries.

'I want to meet with you and discuss the situation,' Leah temporized.

'You mean discuss terms of surrender?'

'Yes.' She practically choked getting the word out. He must have known, darn him, for a low, intimate laugh sounded in her ear.

'You did that very well,' he approved. 'See? Giving in isn't so bad.'

'Yes, it is,' she assured him. 'You try it some time and you'll know what I mean.'

'No, you handle it much better than I would. All you need is a little more practice.'

Married to him, she didn't doubt she'd get it, either. 'Where are you staying?' she asked, deliberately changing the subject. She knew when to give up on a losing hand. 'Should I meet you there?'

'I'm in Houston. And no, I don't expect you to drive that far. We'll meet tomorrow. Noon. The line-shack.'

She caught her breath in disbelief. 'That's not funny, Hunter!'

'It wasn't meant to be.' All trace of amusement vanished from his voice, his tone acquiring a sharp, cutting edge. 'I'm dead serious. Tomorrow meet me at the line-shack at noon. Just like before. See that you make it this time. There won't be any second chances.'

'There weren't eight years ago. Why should this occasion be any different?'

'It will be different,' he promised. 'You'd be smart to realize that right from the start.'

'Fine. You've made your point and I realize it. Things will be different.'

'Very good, Leah. There's hope for you yet.'

She clamped down on her temper, determined not to be provoked. 'So, let's meet at the ranch-house instead. Okay? Hunter?' But she spoke into a dead phone. So much for not being provoked. She was thoroughly provoked.

Slowly she hung up. This did not bode well for their future together. Not well at all. She reached for her list. She wouldn't have that disaster at the line-shack held over her head like the sword of Damocles for the rest of her life. She'd done all the explaining she intended to do, but apparently he had more to say. Well, this meeting would end it once and for all. She wouldn't spend the rest of her life paying for something that, though her ultimate responsibility, wasn't her fault.

Early the next morning she headed for the south pasture to pay a visit to Dreamseeker, the stallion she'd recently acquired. At the fence she whistled, low and piercing, waiting for the familiar whickered response. From the concealing stand of cottonwoods he came, a coal-black stallion, racing across the grass. He danced to a stop ten yards from the fence, pawing at the ground and shaking his mane.

'You don't fool me,' she called to him. 'You want it. I know you do. All you have to do is come and take it.' She held out her hand so he could see the lumps of sugar she'd brought him.

Without further hesitation he charged the fence, but she didn't flinch. Her hand remained rock-steady. Skidding to a halt beside her, the horse ducked his head into her hand and snatched the sugar from her palm. Then he nipped her fingers—not hard, just enough to establish dominance. With a snort, he spun around and galloped across the pasture.

She cradled her palm, refusing to show her hurt. She wouldn't let herself be hurt. It was an indulgence that she couldn't afford. She'd made her decision—a decision that would protect the stallion, protect her ranch, and protect all the wounded creatures she'd gathered safely beneath her wing.

She also understood why Dreamseeker had bitten her. He'd done it to prove that he was still free—free to choose, free to approach or flee. It saddened her, because she knew he lived a lie. They had that in common.

For, no matter how hard they tried, neither was truly free.

Not any more.

Leaving the fence, she saddled a horse and rode to the line-shack. The spring weather had taken a turn for the worse, becoming every bit as hot and humid as that fateful day eight years ago. A sullen mugginess weighted the air, filled it with the threat of a thunderstorm. Leah shuddered. The similarities between then and now were more than she cared to contemplate.

At the line-shack she ground-hitched her gelding. Hunter hadn't arrived yet and she stood outside, reluctant to enter the cabin... reluctant to face any more memories. She'd avoided this place for eight long years. Thanks to Hunter she couldn't avoid it any longer. Setting her chin, she crossed to the door and thrust it open.

She stepped cautiously inside, looking around in disbelief. Everything was spotless. A table, two chairs, a bed—everything in its place. A thin layer of dust was the only visible sign of neglect. Someone had gone to great pains to restore the shack. But who? And why?

'Reliving old memories?'

Leah whirled around. 'Hunter! You startled me.'

He filled the threshold, a blackened silhouette that blocked the sun and caused the walls to close in around them. 'You shouldn't be so easily startled.'

Searching for something to say, she gestured to indicate the cabin. 'It's changed. For some reason I thought the place would have fallen down by now.'

He shrugged. 'You can't run a ranch this size without working line-shacks. The men need someplace to hole up when they're working this far out. Allowing it to fall into ruin would be counterproductive.'

She could feel the tension building between them, despite his air of casual indifference. She wouldn't be able to handle this confrontation for long. Best to get it over with—and fast. She turned and faced him. Unfortunately that only served to heighten her awareness. 'Why did you want to meet here?' she asked, taking the offensive.

'To annoy you.'

Her mouth tightened. 'You succeeded. Was that your only reason?'

'No. I could have had you drive to Houston and negotiate on my turf. But, considering our history...' He shrugged, relaxing against the doorjamb.

He tucked his thumbs into his belt-loops, his jeans hugging his lean hips and clinging to the powerful muscles of his thighs and buttocks. She shouldn't stare, shouldn't remember the times he'd shed his jeans and shirt, exposing his coppery skin to her gaze. But it proved next to impossible to resist the old memories.

He'd had a magnificent physique, something that clearly hadn't changed with time. If anything, his shoulders had broadened, his features had sharpened, becoming more tautly defined. How she wished their circumstances were different, that she didn't fear he'd use her attraction to achieve his goal...to gain his revenge.

Desperately, she forced her attention back to the issue at hand. 'Negotiating here is just as much to your advantage. Dredging up the old memories, playing on my guilt, is supposed to give you added leverage, is that it?'

'Yes. I play to win. You'd be wise to learn that now.'

She ground her teeth in frustration. 'And if I don't?'

He smiled. 'You will. We've come full circle, you and I. We're back where we left off. But nothing's the same as it was. You've changed. I've changed.' He added significantly, 'And our situation has changed.'

'How has it changed?' she asked with sudden curiosity. 'How have you changed? What did you do after you left here?'

He hesitated, and for a minute she thought he wouldn't answer. Then he said, 'I finished my education, for a start. Then I worked twenty-four hours a day building my...fortune.'

'You succeeded, I assume?' she pressed.

'You could say that.'

'That's it? That's all you have to say—you got an education and made your fortune?'

He shrugged. 'That's it.'

She stared at him suspiciously, wondering what he was concealing. Because she didn't doubt for a minute that he hadn't told her everything. What had he left out? And, more importantly, *why*? 'Why so mysterious?' she demanded, voicing her concerns. 'What are you hiding?'

He straightened. 'Still trying to call the shots, Leah? You better get past that, pronto.'

'It's my ranch,' she protested. 'Of course I'm still calling the shots.'

He shook his head. 'It may be your ranch, but I'm the one who'll be in charge. Are we clear on that?'

'No, we're not clear on that!' she asserted vehemently. 'In fact, we're not clear on anything. For one thing, I won't have our past thrown in my face day after day. I won't spend the rest of my life apologizing for what happened.'

'I have no intention of bringing it up again. But I wanted to make it plain, so there's no doubt in your mind. I won't have you claiming later that I didn't warn you.'

She eyed him warily. 'Warn me about what?'

'You've been managing this ranch for over seven years and you've almost run it into the ground. Now I'm supposed to come in and save it. And I will. But you're going to have to understand and accept that I'm in charge. What I say goes. I won't have you questioning me in front of the hired help or second-guessing my decisions. You're going to have to trust me. Implicitly. Without question. And that's going to start here and now.'

'You've been gone a lot of years. It isn't reasonable——'

He grabbed his shirtsleeve and ripped it with one brutal yank, the harsh sound of rending cotton stemming her flow of words. 'You see that scar?' A long, ragged silver line streaked up his forearm.

She swallowed, feeling the blood drain from her face. 'I see it.'

'I got it when the sheriff helped me through that window.' He jerked his head toward the south wall. 'I have another on my inner thigh. One of Lomax's deputies tried to make a point with his spur. He almost succeeded. I broke my collarbone and a couple of ribs on the door here.' He shoved at the casing and it wobbled. 'Still isn't square. Seems I did leave my mark, after all.'

She felt sick. How could her father and Sheriff Lomax have been so cruel? Had Hunter really been such a threat to them? 'Are you doing this for revenge?' she asked in a low voice. 'Trying to get control of the ranch because of how Dad treated you and because I wouldn't go away with you?'

'Believe what you want, but understand this...' He leaned closer, his words cold and harsh. 'I got dragged off this land once. It won't happen again. If you can't accept that, sell out. But if you marry me, don't expect a partnership. I don't work by committee.'

'Those are your conditions? What you say goes? That's it?'

He inclined his head. 'That just about covers it.'

'It doesn't come close to covering it,' she protested. 'I have a few conditions of my own.'

'I didn't doubt it for a minute.'

She pulled the list she'd compiled from her pocket and, ignoring his quiet laugh, asked, 'What about my employees? They've been with me for a long time. What sort of guarantee are you offering that changes won't be made?'

'I'm not making any guarantees. If they can pull their weight, they stay. It's as simple as that.'

She stared in alarm. Pull their weight? Every last one of them pulled his or her own weight... to the best of their ability. But that might not be good enough to suit Hunter's high standards. Patrick had a bad leg and wasn't as fast or strong as another foreman might be.

And what about the Arroyas? Mateo and his wife Inez would have starved if she hadn't taken them in. Inez, as competent a housekeeper as she was, had six children to care for. Leah had always insisted that the children's needs come first, even at the expense of routine chores. Would Hunter feel the same way? And Mateo was a wonder with horses but, having lost his arm in a car accident, certain jobs were difficult for him—tasks she performed in his stead.

'But——'

'Are you already questioning my judgement?' he asked softly.

She stirred uneasily. 'No, not exactly. I'd just appreciate some sort of guarantee that these people won't be fired.' She saw his expression close over. 'I'm responsible for them,' she forced herself to explain. 'They couldn't find work anywhere else. At least, not easily.'

'I'm not an unfair or unreasonable man,' he said in a clipped voice. 'They won't be terminated without due cause.'

It was the best she'd get from him. 'And Grandmother Rose?'

A tiny flicker of anger burned in his eyes. 'Do you think I don't know how much Hampton Homestead means to her? Believe me, I'm well aware of the extent she'd go to to keep the ranch.'

Her fingers tightened on the list. 'You don't expect her to move?'

She could tell from his expression that she'd offended him, and she suspected that it was a slight he wouldn't soon forgive. 'As much as the idea appeals, it isn't my intention to turn her from her home,' he said curtly. 'What's next on your list?'

Taking him at his word, she plunged on. 'I want a prenuptial agreement that states that in the event of a divorce I get to keep the ranch.'

'There won't be a divorce.'

She lifted her chin. 'Then you won't object to the agreement, will you?'

He ran a hand across the back of his neck, clearly impatient with her requests. 'We'll let our lawyers hammer out the finer details. I refuse to start our marriage discussing an imaginary divorce.'

She wouldn't get any more of a concession than that. 'Agreed.'

'Next?'

She took a deep breath. This final item would be the trickiest of all. 'I won't sleep with you.'

His smile was derisive. 'That's an unrealistic request and you damned well know it.'

'It's not. I——'

He cut her off without hesitation. 'This is going to be a real marriage—in every sense of the word. We sleep together, drink, eat and make love together.'

'Not a chance,' she protested, her voice taking on an edge of desperation even she couldn't mistake. 'You wanted control of the ranch and you're getting that. I won't be part of the bargain. I won't barter myself.'

Sardonic amusement touched his expression. 'You will and you'll like it,' he informed her softly. 'I know you too well not to make it good for you.'

'You knew an inexperienced eighteen-year-old girl,' she declared passionately. 'You know nothing about the person I've become. You know nothing of my hopes or dreams or desires. And you never will.'

'Another challenge?' He moved closer. 'Shall we settle that here and now? The bed's a little narrow, but it'll do. I guarantee you won't be disappointed.'

She took a hasty step back, knowing there was no-where to escape should he decide to put action to words. 'You bastard,' she whispered. 'I won't be forced.'

'I don't use force. I don't have to.' For a horrifying second she thought he'd prove it, that he'd sweep her up without regard and carry her to the bed. That he'd scatter her resistance like so much chaff before the breeze. Then he relaxed, though his gaze remained guarded and watchful. 'What about children?' he asked unexpectedly. 'Or are they off your list, too?'

Events had proceeded so swiftly that she hadn't given the possibility any thought at all. 'Do you want children?' she asked uncertainly.

He cocked his head to one side, eyeing her with an uncomfortable intensity. 'Do you? Or, should I say, do you want *my* children?'

'Once, that was all I dreamed about,' she confessed in a low voice.

'And now?'

She looked at him, fighting her nervousness. 'Yes, I want children.'

'You won't get them if I agree to your condition. Cross it off your list, Leah. It's not a negotiable point.'

She didn't want to concede defeat, didn't want to agree to give herself to him without love, without commitment. But he'd left her without choice. 'Hunter, please...'

He closed the distance between them. Cupping her head, he tilted her face up to his. 'We'll make love, you and I, and we'll have children. Plenty of them. Though chances are they won't be blue-eyed blondes. Can you live with that?'

'I'm not my father. I know you don't believe it, but it's true. Do you really think I could love my child less because he's dark...' she dared to feather her fingers through his hair '...instead of fair?'

He caught her hand and drew it to his scarred arm, her pale skin standing out starkly against his sun-bronzed tan. 'It matters to some.'

'Not to me. It never mattered to me.'

He nodded, apparently accepting her words at face value. 'Any more conditions?' he asked, flicking her list with a finger.

'No,' she admitted. 'But you'd better know up-front—I can't promise I won't argue with you. I love this ranch And I'll do all I can to protect the people on it.'

He shook his head. 'That's my job now.'

'That doesn't mean I won't worry.'

'Worrying is also my job,' he informed her gravely.

She nodded. That left only one last decision to be made. 'About the wedding...'

'I want to marry by the end of the week. Tell me where and when and I'll be there. Just make sure it's no later than Saturday.'

'So soon?' she asked in dismay. 'That's less than a week.'

'Are you having second thoughts?'

'Constantly. But it won't change anything. I won't sell and I can't save the ranch unless I marry you. But a wedding... There's a lot to be done and not much time to do it in.'

'Find the time.' He tugged her more fully into his arms. 'I have to go,' he said, and kissed her.

His touch drove out all thought and reason, banishing the ghosts that lingered from that other time and place. And no matter how hard she wanted to oppose him, to keep a small piece of herself safe and protected, he stripped her of all resistance with consummate ease. Deepening the kiss, he cupped her breast, teasing the tender peak through the thin cotton. And she let him... let him touch her as he wished, let him explore where he willed, let him drive her toward that sweet crest she'd once shared exclusively with him.

For a moment Leah was able to pretend that she meant something to him again, that he really cared for her more than he cared for her ranch. But as hard as she tried to lose herself in his embrace, the knowledge that this was in all probability a game of revenge intruded, and finally drove her from his arms.

He released her without protest. 'Call me with the details,' he instructed, and headed for the door. 'We'll need to get the license as soon as possible.'

'There's one last thing,' she suddenly remembered. He paused, waiting for her to continue and, almost stumbling over the words, she said, 'Conrad... Conrad Michaels. He retired.' Hunter didn't say anything, prompting her to state her concerns more openly. 'Are you responsible for his retirement?'

'Yes.'

She'd suspected as much, but it still shocked her to hear him admit it. '*Why?*' He didn't reply. Instead he walked outside, forcing her to give chase. Without breaking stride, he gathered up his buckskin's reins and mounted. She clung to his saddle-skirt, hindering his departure, desperate for an answer. 'Hunter, please. Tell me why. Why did you force Conrad to retire?'

After a momentary hesitation he leaned across the horn, fixing her with hard black eyes. 'Because he put you at risk.'

Alarmed, she took a step back. 'What are you talking about?'

'I'm talking about the ad.'

'But I placed the ad, not Conrad.'

'He knew about it, and not only did he not try and stop it he encouraged you to go ahead with it while in his capacity as your banker.' His face might have been carved from granite. 'You still don't have a clue as to how dangerous that was, do you?'

'We were very selective,' she defended.

'You were a fool,' he stated succinctly. 'You might as well have painted a bullseye on your backside, stuck your pinfeathers in the air and proclaimed it open hunting season. Count yourself lucky that you and that old harridan of a grandmother weren't murdered in your beds.'

'So you had Conrad fired.'

'I wanted to!' he bit out. 'Believe me, more than anything I wanted to have him fired for planting such a criminal suggestion in your head. Considering he's an old family friend, I let him off easy. I agreed to an early retirement.'

A sudden thought struck her. 'If you're that powerful—powerful enough to force Conrad's retirement—what do you need with this ranch?' She spoke urgently. 'It has to be small potatoes to you. Why are you doing this, Hunter?'

A grim smile touched his mouth and he yanked the brim of his stetson low over his brow. 'That, my sweet bride-to-be, is one question I have no intention of answering.'

And with that he rode off into the approaching storm, the dark, angry clouds sweeping across the sky ahead of him, full of flash and fury. A portent of things to come? Leah wondered uneasily. Or a promise?

CHAPTER FOUR

WITH only five days to prepare for her wedding, Leah realized that the simplest solution would be to hold the ceremony at the ranch. She also decided to make it an evening affair and keep it small, inviting only her closest friends and employees.

Her reasons were twofold. She didn't think she could handle a day-long celebration—the mere thought of celebrating a marriage that was in all actuality a business deal struck her as vulgar. And by holding an evening ceremony they'd entertain the guests for dinner and it would be over quickly. No fuss, no muss.

Her grandmother didn't offer a single word of argument in regard to Leah's wedding-plans. On only one matter did she remain adamant. She insisted that Leah invite Conrad Michaels. 'He's a close friend and should give you away. If that makes Hunter uncomfortable, that's his tough luck.'

'I don't think it's Hunter who will feel uncomfortable,' Leah observed wryly. 'Let me call Conrad and see what he wants to do. If he chooses to decline, I won't pressure him.'

As it turned out, Conrad sounded quite anxious to attend. 'I'd appreciate the opportunity to improve my relationship with Hunter,' he confessed. 'I deserved every harsh word he dished out, and then some.'

'Harsh word?' she repeated in alarm. 'What did he say?'

After a long, awkward silence, Conrad admitted, 'Oh, this and that. Let's just describe the conversation as strained and forget I ever mentioned it. He did make several valid points, though—particularly about your ad.'

So Hunter *had* taken Conrad to task about that. She'd wondered. 'What points?' she questioned.

'I never should have encouraged you to advertise for a husband,' came the prompt reply. 'Looking back, I realize it was foolish in the extreme. It didn't occur to me until Hunter suggested the possibility, but a crazy person could have responded and we wouldn't have known until too late. I never would have forgiven myself if anything had happened to you.'

Unfortunately, something *had* happened. Hunter had answered the ad. To her disgust, she seemed to be the only one to appreciate the irony of that fact. 'It's all worked out for the best,' she lied through her teeth. 'So don't worry about it.' Securing Conrad's agreement to give her away, she ended the conversation and hung up.

The next two days passed in a whirl of confusion. Leah spent her time deciding on caterers and flowers, food and decorations, and obtaining the all-important wedding-license. Finally she threw her hands in the air and dropped the entire mess in the laps of her grandmother and Inez Arroya. 'You decide,' she begged. 'Just keep it simple.'

'But, *señorita, por favor...*' Inez protested. 'The wedding, it should be perfect. What if we make a mistake? You will be very unhappy. Don't you care?'

Didn't she care? Leah turned away. She cared too much. That was the problem. How could she plan for the wedding of her dreams when the ceremony on Friday would be anything but? 'Whatever you decide will be perfect,' she said flatly. 'Just remember. Keep it simple.'

'What about your dress?' Rose reminded, before Leah could escape. 'You've deliberately ignored that minor detail, haven't you?'

'I thought I could pick something up on Thursday,' Leah said, refusing to acknowledge the truth in her grandmother's words.

But on this one point Rose became surprisingly obstinate. 'Oh, no, you don't, my girl. I have the perfect gown for you. Your mother wore it for her wedding and it's the most unusual dress I've ever laid eyes on. It's packed away in the attic, if memory serves. Find it and see if it fits. Though considering how much you resemble your momma, I'd be surprised if it didn't.'

Reluctantly, Leah obeyed. It took a good bit of searching, but she eventually found a huge, sealed box with her mother's name and the date of her wedding scrawled across one end. Wiping away the dust, she carried it downstairs. She didn't return to the kitchen, needing a moment alone in the privacy of her bedroom to examine her mother's wedding-dress. Closing and locking the door, she settled on the floor and carefully cut open the box.

Lifting off the lid, she sank back on her heels, her breath catching in her throat. Her grandmother had been right. It was the most unusual dress Leah had ever seen. Her mother had been a teacher of medieval history and her dress reflected her obsession, right down to the filmy veil with its accompanying silver circlet. It was beautiful and romantic, the sort of dress young women dreamed of wearing.

And Leah hated it with a passion that left her shaking.

The dress promised joy and happiness, not the businesslike relationship soon to be hers. The dress promised a lifetime of laughter and companionship, not the strife and friction that was all she could expect from an empty marriage. But most of all the dress promised everlasting love, not the bitterness and pain that consumed her husband-to-be. She ached for the future the dress suggested, but knew it could never be hers.

This marriage would be an act of vengeance, and she nothing more than a pawn in Hunter's game. It was a way to even up old scores for the abuse he'd suffered at her father's hands. Soon he would be master of his enemy's castle and she'd be at his mercy. How long would it take before he had it all? How long before he controlled not just the ranch but her heart and soul as well?

How long before he had his final revenge?

Gently she replaced the lid of the box. She couldn't wear her mother's wedding-gown. It wouldn't be right. It would be...sacrilegious. She'd drive into town and find a chic ivory suit that spoke of modern marriages and easy divorces. And instead of a gauzy veil she'd purchase a pert little hat that no one would dream of referring to as 'romantic'.

Not giving herself time to reconsider, she shoved the box beneath her bed. Then she ran outside and whistled for Dreamseeker, needing just for an instant to feel what her stallion felt—free and wild and unfettered. But the horse didn't respond to her call. And in that instant Leah felt more alone than she ever had before in her life.

'What do you mean, I can't wear the suit?' Leah demanded of Inez. 'Why can't I? Where is it?'

'*Arrunina, señorita. Lo siento.*'

'Ruined! How?'

'The iron, it burned your dress.'

'But the dress didn't need ironing.'

The housekeeper looked close to tears. 'I'm sorry. I wanted everything to be perfect for your special day. I was excited and...' She wrung her hands. 'Forgive me.'

'It's all right, Inez,' Leah said with a sigh. 'But I get married in less than an hour. What am I supposed to wear? I can't go down in this.' She indicated the wisps of silk and lace beneath her robe.

'Señora Rose, she suggests the dress of your *madre*. *Es perfecta, sí?*'

Leah closed her eyes, understanding finally dawning. Of all the conniving, meddling, devious... Before she could gather the courage to yank the first outfit that came to hand from her closet, Inez draped the wedding-dress across the bed. In a swirl of featherlight pleats the silvery-white silk billowed over the quilted spread, the hem trailing to the floor.

In that instant, Leah was lost. She touched the form-fitting bodice—a corset-like affair, decorated with a honeycombed network of tiny seed pearls and silver thread—thinking that it resembled nothing more than a gossamer-fine cobweb. It really was an enchanting gown. And it had been her mother's.

Knowing further arguing would prove fruitless, Leah allowed the housekeeper to help her into the gown. It fit perfectly, as she'd known it would. Thin white ribbons accentuated the puffed sleeves, the deep, flowing points almost brushing the carpet.

'The belt, *señorita*,' Inez said.

The housekeeper lifted the silver linked chain from the bed and wound it twice around Leah's waist and hips, the pearl-studded clasp fastening in front. The ends of the chain, decorated with tiny unicorn charms, fell to her knees, the links whispering like golden-toned chimes with her every movement.

'For purity,' the housekeeper murmured, touching the unicorns.

'Not terribly appropriate,' Leah said in a dry voice. 'I wonder if it's too late to change them.'

'You are pure of heart, which is all that counts,' Inez maintained stoutly. 'I will do your hair now. You wish to wear it loose?'

'I thought I'd braid it.'

'Oh, no, *señorita*. Perhaps a compromise?' Without waiting for a response, she swiftly braided two narrow sections on each side of Leah's face, threading a silver cord into each as she went. Pulling the braids to the back of Leah's head, the housekeeper pinned them into an intricate knot.

'That looks very nice,' Leah admitted.

'We leave the rest loose,' Inez said, brushing the hip-length curls into some semblance of order. Finally she draped the veil over Leah's hair and affixed the circlet to her brow. Stepping back, she clasped her hands and sighed. '*Qué hermosa*. Señor Hunter, he is a lucky man.'

Leah didn't reply. What could she say? That luck had nothing to do with it, unless it was bad luck? Her bad luck. 'How much time is left?' she asked instead.

'A few minutes, no more. Señor Michaels is waiting for you at the bottom of the stairs.'

'I'm ready,' she announced. She picked up her bouquet of freshly picked wild flowers—courtesy of the Arroya children—and kissed Inez's cheek. 'Thank you for all your help. Go on downstairs. I'll follow in a minute.'

The door closed behind the housekeeper and, finally alone, Leah glanced at the stranger in the mirror. What would Hunter think? she wondered. Would he find her gown ridiculous? Attractive? Would her appearance even matter to him? She shut her eyes and whispered an urgent prayer, a prayer that Hunter might some day find happiness and peace in their marriage...that maybe, just maybe, he'd find love. Slightly more relaxed, she turned away from the mirror. She couldn't delay any longer. It was time to go.

As she descended the stairs, the pleated skirt of her dress swirled around her like wisps of silver fog. Conrad waited at the bottom. He looked up at her, and his reaction was all she could have asked. He stared in stunned disbelief, his mouth agape.

'Leah,' he murmured gruffly, his voice rough and choked. 'My dear, you're a vision. You make me wish...'

She traversed the final few steps, a small smile playing about her mouth. 'Wish what?'

'Wish that I hadn't so foolishly encouraged you to place that ad,' he confessed. 'Are you sure this marriage is what you want? It's not too late to change your mind.'

She didn't hesitate for an instant. 'It's much too late and you know it. Not that it matters. I haven't changed my mind.'

He nodded without argument. 'Then this is it.' He offered his elbow. 'Shall we?'

She slipped her hand into the crook of his arm and walked with him to the great room, an area used for entertaining that stretched the full length of the ranch-house. It was her turn to stare in disbelief. Huge urns of flowers filled the room, their delicate perfume heavy in the air. And everywhere was the radiant glow of candlelight, not a single light-bulb disturbing the soft, romantic scene.

Her gaze flew to the far side of the room where Hunter stood, and her heart pounded in her breast. The wrangler she'd always known had disappeared and in his place stood a man who wore a tuxedo with the same ease as he wore jeans. She'd never seen him look so sophisticated, nor so aloof.

His hair reflected the candlelight, gleaming with blue-black highlights, and his eyes glittered like obsidian, burning with the fire of passion held barely in check. Despite that, he remained detached from his surroundings, the high, taut cheekbones and squared chin set in cool, distant lines.

The sudden hush that greeted her arrival drew his attention and his gaze settled on her with piercing intensity. Her hands tightened around her bouquet, sudden fear turning her fingers to ice. With that single glance his air of detachment fell away and his expression came alive, frightening in its ferocity. He looked like a warrior who'd fixed his sights on his next conquest. And she was that prize. It took all her willpower not to gather up her skirts and run.

Conrad started to move and she had no choice but to fall into step beside him. In keeping with the medieval theme, soft stringed instruments played in the background. She focused on Hunter, barely aware of her passage down the aisle, even more dimly aware of Conrad releasing her and stepping back. But every part of her leapt to life the instant Hunter took possession of her hand.

The minister began the ceremony. She didn't hear a word he said; she didn't even remember making her marriage vows. Afterward, she wondered if she'd actually promised to obey her husband or if the minister had thoughtfully omitted that rather antiquated phrase. She didn't doubt that Hunter would refresh her memory at some point.

The ring he eventually slid on her finger felt strange on her hand, the unaccustomed weight a visible reminder of all the changes soon to come. She stared at the ring for a long time, studying the simple scrollwork and wondering why he'd chosen such an interesting design. Did it have any particular significance or had it been a simple matter of expediency?

'Leah.' Hunter's soft prompt captured her full attention.

She glanced up at him in bewilderment. 'Did I miss something?' she asked. Quiet laughter broke out among the guests and brought a flush to her cheeks. Even Hunter grinned, and she found herself riveted by that smile, aware that it had been eight long years since she'd last seen it.

'We've just been pronounced man and wife,' he told her. 'Which means...' He swung her into his embrace and lowered his head. 'It's time to kiss the bride.'

And he proceeded to do so with great expertise and thoroughness. It was her first kiss as his wife and the warm caress held all the magic she could desire. She was lost in his embrace, swept up in the moment. Yet, as intensely as she craved his touch, she longed to resist with an equal intensity. She couldn't bear the knowledge that this whole situation was nothing more than Hunter's way of gaining control of her ranch... and of her.

At long last he released her, his look of satisfaction stirring a flash of anger. Fortunately her irritation swiftly disappeared beneath the flurry of congratulations from the press of friends and employees. By the time Inez announced dinner, she'd fully regained her composure.

Like the great room, the dining-room glowed with candlelight, flowers running the length of the oak table and overflowing the side tables and buffet. To her relief she and Hunter were seated at opposite ends, though as dinner progressed she discovered her relief short-lived. Throughout the meal she felt his gaze fixed on her. And as the evening passed her awareness of him grew, along with an unbearable tension.

As the caterers cleared away the final course, Hunter rose, glass in hand. 'A toast,' he announced. Silence descended and all eyes turned in his direction.

'A toast for the bride?' Conrad questioned.

'A toast to my wife.' Hunter lifted the glass. 'To the most beautiful woman I've ever known. May all her dreams come true... and may they be worth the price she pays for them.'

There was a momentary confused silence and then the guests lifted their glasses in tribute, murmuring, 'Hear, hear.'

Slowly Leah stood, well aware of the double edge to Hunter's toast. Lifting her own glass in salute, she said, 'And to my husband. The answer to all my dreams.' And let him make what he wished of that, she thought, drinking deeply.

The party broke up not long after. Rose had arranged to stay with friends for the weekend and all the staff had been given the days off as a paid vacation. Only Patrick would remain, to care for the animals. But, knowing her foreman's sensitivity, he'd make himself scarce. They wouldn't see any sign of him until Monday morning.

Sending the last few guests on their way, Leah stood with Hunter in the front hall. The tension between them threatened to overwhelm her and she twisted her hands together, feeling again the unexpected weight of her wedding-ring.

She glanced at it and asked the question that had troubled her during the ceremony. 'Did you choose it or...?'

'I chose it. Did you really think I'd leave it to my secretary to take care of?'

'I didn't even know you had a secretary,' she confessed. 'What do... did you do?'

He hesitated. 'Mostly I worked as a sort of trouble-shooter for a large consortium, taking care of problem situations no one else could handle.'

She drifted toward the great room, snuffing candles as she went. 'I imagine you'd be good at that sort of thing. What made you decide to give it up and return to ranching?'

'What makes you think I've quit?' he asked from directly behind.

Startled, she spun around, her gown flaring out around her. 'Haven't you?'

'They know to call if something urgent comes up. I'll find a way to fit it in.' He drew her away from a low bracket of candles. 'Be careful. I'd hate to see this go up in flames.'

'It was my mother's,' she admitted self-consciously. 'I wasn't sure whether you'd like it.'

His voice deepened. 'I like it.'

She caught her breath, finally managed to say, 'You still haven't answered my question.'

'What question?' A lazy gleam sparked in his eyes and she knew his thoughts were elsewhere. Precisely where, she didn't care to contemplate.

'Why,' she persisted, 'if you had such a good job, did you decide to come back?'

'Let's just call it unfinished business and leave it at that. Do you really want to start an argument tonight?'

She glanced at him in alarm. 'Would it? Start an argument, I mean?'

'Without a doubt.' He pinched out the remaining few candles, leaving them in semi-darkness, the night enclosing them in a cloak of intimacy. 'I have a wedding-gift for you.' He picked up a small package tucked among a basket of flowers and handed it to her.

She took it, staring in wonder. 'A wedding-gift?'

'Open it.'

Carefully, she ripped the paper from the jewelry box and removed the lid. Beneath a layer of cotton lay an odd blue stone with a thin gold band wrapped around it, securing it to a delicate herringbone chain. 'It's just like yours!' she exclaimed, tears starting to her eyes.

The only identifying article left with Hunter at the orphanage had been the strange gold-encased stone identical to the one he'd duplicated for a wedding-present. He'd worn it like a talisman all the time she'd known him, though he'd never been able to trace its origin successfully.

'I thought a gold chain a better choice than the leather thong I use.'

'Thank you. It's beautiful.' She handed him the box and turned her back to him. 'Will you put it on?' She lifted her hair and veil out of the way while he fastened the chain around her neck. The stone nestled between her breasts, cool and heavy against her skin.

Before she realized what he intended, Hunter turned her around and swung her into his arms. She clutched at his shoulders, her heart beating frantically, knowing that she couldn't delay the inevitable any longer. He strode across the entrance hall and climbed the stairs, booting open the door to the master bedroom.

She started to protest, but stopped when she saw the candles and flowers that festooned the room. At a guess, it was more of her grandmother's fine handiwork. This time, though, Leah approved. Giving them the master bedroom was Rose's tacit acknowledgement of Hunter's position in the household.

'Where's Rose's room?' he asked, as though reading her mind.

'Downstairs. She had a private wing built when my father married. She said the only smart way for an ex-tended family to cohabit was to live apart.'

A reluctant smile touched his mouth. 'There may be hope for our relationship yet.'

He set her down, his smile fading, a dark, intense expression growing in his eyes. He removed the circlet from her brow and swept the veil from her hair. It floated to the floor, a gauzy slip of silver against the burgundy carpet.

He stepped back. 'Take off the dress. I don't want to rip it.'

Fumbling awkwardly with the belt links, she unfastened the chain at her waist and placed it among the flowers on the walnut bureau. She slipped off her heels, wondering why removing her shoes always made her feel small and vulnerable. Finally she gathered the hem of her gown and slowly lifted it to her waist.

The next instant she felt Hunter's hands beside her own, easing the dress over her head. He laid it across a chair and turned back to her. She stood in the center of the room, horribly self-conscious in the sheer wisps of silk and lace that were her only covering.

'Hunter,' she whispered. 'I don't think I'm ready for this.'

'Relax,' he murmured. 'There's no rush. We have all the time in the world.' He approached, wrapping her in his embrace. 'Remember how good it was between us?'

She clung to his jacket lapel. 'But we're not the same people any more. Our... our feelings have changed.'

'Some things never change. And this is one of them.' His eyes were so black, full of heat and hunger, his face, tight and drawn, reflecting his desire. He lifted her against him, tracing the length of her jaw with the edge of his thumb.

She shuddered beneath the delicate caress. He'd always been incredibly tender with her, a lover who combined a sensitive awareness of a woman's needs with a forceful passion that had made loving him an experience she'd never forgotten. It would be so easy to succumb, to be swept into believing he loved her still—a fantasy she found all too appealing.

'I can make it so good for you,' he said, his mouth drifting from her earlobe to the tiny pulse throbbing in her neck. 'Let me show you.' He found the clasp of her bra and unhooked it, sliding the silk from her body.

She closed her eyes, her breathing shallow and rapid. He didn't lie. She knew from experience that making love to him would be wonderful. It was the morning after that concerned her, when she'd have to face the knowledge that he'd come one step closer to achieving his goal—of winning both the ranch and her. His hand closed over her breast and her heart pounded beneath the warmth of his palm. For an endless instant she hung in the balance between conceding defeat and allowing her emotions free rein, or fighting for what mattered most. Because if she couldn't protect *herself* from his determined assault, how could she ever expect to protect the ranch and all those who depended on her?

She shifted within his grasp. 'It's too soon,' she protested in a low voice.

'We'll take it slow.' He traced her curves with a callused hand, scalding her with his touch. 'We can always stop.' But we won't want to. The words lay unvoiced between them, his thoughts as clear to her as if he'd spoken them aloud, and she shuddered.

Stepping back, he stripped off his jacket and tie. Ripping open the buttons of his shirt, he swept her into his arms and carried her to the petal-adorned bed. Once there he lowered her to the soft mattress and followed her down.

His fingers sank into her hair, filling his hands with long silvery curls. 'I've wanted to do this ever since I saw that picture of you,' he muttered.

She stirred uneasily. 'What picture?'

He tensed, and for a long moment neither of them moved. Her question had caught him unawares and she struggled to focus on it, to figure out why he'd reacted so strongly. He'd seen a recent picture of her. The knowledge was inescapable and she withdrew slightly, confused, questions hammering at her brain. Where and when had he seen the photo... in the study, perhaps? If so, why the strange reaction?

'The picture on your father's desk,' he explained quietly. 'It shows you with long hair.'

'It was shorter when you worked here.'

'Yeah, well. I like it long.'

But the mood had been broken and she rolled away from him, drawing her knees up against her chest. There was more to his idle comment than she had the strength or energy to analyze. 'Hunter,' she said in a low tone. 'I can't.'

'It's only natural to feel nervous,' he said in a cool voice, making no attempt to touch her.

'It's not just nerves.' She swept up the sheet, wrapping herself in its concealing folds. Shoving her hair back over her shoulders, she met his watchful gaze. 'You've gotten your way, Hunter. We're married and there's no going back. You said yourself that we have all the time in the world. Why rush this part of it and risk damaging our relationship?'

A muscle leapt in his jaw. 'You think making love will damage our relationship?'

She caught her lower lip between her lip and nodded. 'It will if we're not both ready for this. And, in all honesty, I'm not ready.'

'When will you be?' he asked bluntly.

She shrugged uneasily. 'I couldn't say.'

'Give it your best guess. I don't have an infinite amount of patience.'

'That's not what you told me five minutes ago,' she flashed back.

He clasped her shoulders, hauling her close. 'Five minutes ago you were as anxious as I to consummate this marriage. You want me every bit as much as I want you. I know it and you know it.'

'That's lust, not love. And lust isn't enough for me.' Aware of how much she'd inadvertently revealed, she fought free of his hold and scrambled off the bed. 'I . . . I just need a little bit of time, that's all. Can't you understand? Am I asking so much?'

He laughed harshly, running a hand through his hair. 'What will happen between us is inevitable. Tonight, tomorrow or the next night . . . What's the difference?'

She peeked at him through long lashes. 'Forty-eight hours,' she said with a hesitant smile. For a minute she didn't think he'd respond. Then he relaxed, his tension dissipating, and he nodded, though she sensed a strong undercurrent of anger just beneath his surface calm.

'Okay, Leah. I'll wait.' His gaze held a warning. 'Just don't push it. My tolerance has limits.'

'I'm well aware of that.' She backed toward the door. 'I'd like to change.'

'Don't be long.'

Striving for as much dignity as possible, considering that she kept tripping over the sheet, she left Hunter and hurried to her own room. There she stripped off her few remaining clothes. Pawing through her dresser drawers, she pulled out the most modest nightgown she possessed and tugged it on.

Covered from head to toe in yards and yards of baby-fine linen, she sat on the edge of the bed and nibbled on her fingertip. Had she made her situation better or worse? she wondered. She wasn't quite sure. Perhaps it would have been wiser to make love with him and be done with it, regardless of his motivations for marrying her. Only, in her heart of hearts, she knew it wouldn't truly be lovemaking, at least not on his part. It would be sex, pure and not so simple. Or, worse... it would be revenge.

She curled up on the bed, hugging a pillow to her chest. If only he cared. If only he loved her. Her hand closed around his wedding-gift, the talisman he'd so unexpectedly given her. His love would make all the difference in the world. But he no longer felt that way about her. And the sooner she accepted that, the better off she'd be.

But telling herself that didn't prevent a wistful tear from sliding down her cheek.

CHAPTER FIVE

LEAH stirred just as dawn broke the horizon. Confused by the unexpected weight pinning her legs to the mattress, she turned her head and found herself face to face with Hunter—a sleeping Hunter. It brought her fully awake. She risked a quick glance around, confirming her suspicions. So she hadn't dreamed it. She was back in the master bedroom.

Vaguely she remembered Hunter coming to her old room where she'd drifted off on top of the bed, a pillow clutched to her breast. He'd gently pried it free, and at her drowsy protest rasped, 'We sleep together, wife.' With that, he'd lifted her into his arms and carried her from the room. She hadn't fought. Instead, she'd wound her arms around his neck and snuggled against his chest as though she belonged, as though she never wanted to let go.

When he'd put her into his bed she'd been greeted by the sweet aroma of crushed flowers, followed by a stronger, muskier scent as Hunter had joined her on the mattress. All she recalled after that was a delicious warmth and peace invading her, body and soul, as he'd enclosed her in his embrace, wrapping her in a protective cocoon of strong arms and taut, muscular legs.

She glanced at him again, studying his imposing features with an acute curiosity. Even sleep couldn't blunt his tough, masculine edge, a night's growth of beard only serving to intensify the aura of danger and male aggression that clung to him like a second skin. The sheet skimmed his waist, baring his broad chest to her view,

79

and she drank in the clean, powerful lines, wondered if he slept nude. Somehow she suspected that he did, though she didn't have the nerve to peek.

In all their times together, never had they been able to spend a night in each other's arms. Their joining had been passionate and earth-shattering and the most wondrous experience of her life. But it had also consisted of brief, stolen moments away from the suspicious eyes of her father and grandmother and the other ranch employees.

The irony of their current situation didn't escape her. Years ago she'd have given anything to spend a single night with him. To know, just once, the rapture of greeting the dawn safe and secure within his sheltering hold. Finally given her dearest wish, all she felt was apprehension and dismay—and an overwhelming desire to escape before he awoke.

Cautiously she slipped from his loose grasp and eased off the bed. Only then did she realize that some time during the early morning hours her nightgown had become trapped beneath him, and that he'd entwined her hair in his fingers as though, even in his sleep, he couldn't bear to let her go. Precious moments flew by as she untangled her hair and freed her gown. Gathering up the voluminous skirt, she tiptoed from the room.

A quick stop in the kitchen to grab an apple and a handful of sugar cubes, and she was outside and free. She raced across the dew-laden grass to the south pasture fence, the wind catching her hair and sweeping it into the air behind her like long, silver streamers. Whistling for Dreamseeker, she wondered if she'd ever tame such a wild and willful beast.

He came to her then, bursting across the pasture, a streak of jet against a cornflower-blue sky. Forming a deep pocket for the apple and sugar with the excess material of her nightgown, she awkwardly climbed the fence and sat on the top rail, the thin cotton affording little protection from the splintered wood beneath.

Dreamseeker joined her, snatching greedily at the apple she offered. Not satisfied, he butted her shoulder until she relented and gave him the sugar as well. He waited, muscles quivering, head cocked at an arrogant angle, allowing her to scratch and caress his gleaming coat. She crooned in delight, rubbing his withers, thrilled by his show of trust.

'What the *hell* are you doing?'

Leah didn't know who was more startled, she or Dreamseeker. Springing from her grasp, the horse shot away from the fence, leaving her teetering on the rail. With a cry of alarm, she tumbled to the ground at Hunter's feet, the hem of her gown snagging on a protruding nail. She tugged impatiently at it, the sound of ripping cloth making her wince.

She glared up at him, placing the blame where it belonged—square on his broad shoulders. 'Dammit, Hunter! This is all your fault. What do you mean, sneaking around like that?'

He folded his arms across his chest and lifted an eyebrow. 'Sneaking?'

'Yes, sneaking. You scared Dreamseeker and you scared me.' She shook out her nightgown, lifting the dew-soaked hem clear of the grass. Peering over her shoulder, she searched for the source of the ripping sound. Finding it, she muttered in disgust, 'Just look at the size of that hole.'

'I'm looking.'

The hint of amusement in his voice brought her head around with a jerk. His eyes weren't on the tear but on her. Realization came swiftly. With the sun at her back, the thin cotton she wore might as well have been transparent. And Hunter, his thumbs once again thrust in his belt-loops, was enjoying every minute of the show.

'There are times, Hunter Pryde, when I think I hate you,' she declared vehemently. With that, she grabbed a fistful of skirt, lifted her nightgown to her knees and lit off across the pastureland. She didn't get far.

In two swift strides he overtook her, and swept her clean off her feet. 'Hate me all you want, wife. It won't change a damned thing. The sooner you realize that, the better off you'll be.'

She shrieked in fury, lashing out at him, hampered by yards of damp cotton. Her hair, seeming to have acquired a life of its own, further hindered her efforts, wrapping around her arms and torso in a tangle of unruly silver curls. She stopped struggling, battering him with words instead. 'You don't fool me. You may have married me because it was the only way to get your hands on the ranch, but that doesn't mean you've won. I'll never give in.'

'Won't you?' A hint of sardonic amusement touched his aquiline features. 'We'll see.'

She had to convince him. She had to convince herself. 'You won't win, Hunter. I won't let you!'

'So much passion. So much energy,' he murmured, his arms tightening around her. 'And all of it wasted out here. Why don't we take it inside where we can put it to good use?'

She stiffened, quick to catch his meaning, quicker still to voice her objections. 'You promised. You promised to wait until I was ready. And I'm not ready.'

'No?' His mouth twisted, and a cynical gleam sparked in his jet-black eyes. 'Listen up, wife. It wouldn't take much for me to break that promise. And when I do, count on it, you won't complain for long.'

Without another word he carried her inside. In the front hallway he dumped her on to her feet, forcing her to cling to him while she regained her balance. His biceps were like rock beneath her hands, the breadth of his chest and shoulders an impenetrable wall between her and escape.

'Hunter, let me go,' she whispered, the words an aching plea. She didn't dare look him in the eye, didn't dare see the passion that she knew marked his strong, determined features. If she did, she'd never make it up those steps alone.

'Not a chance.' Then he further destroyed her equilibrium with a single hard, fiery kiss. At last he released her, and she stared at him with wide, anguished eyes. She didn't want him touching her, kissing her, forcing her back to life. She didn't want to feel, to experience anew the pain loving him would bring.

But she suspected that he didn't care what she wanted, or how much he hurt her. He had his own agenda. And she was low on his list of priorities—a minor detail he'd address when he found it convenient.

He snagged the bodice of her nightgown with his finger and tugged her close. 'I warned you last night. I won't wait forever. I catch you running around like this ever again and I won't be responsible for my actions. You hear me?'

She wrenched the gown from his grasp, but all she got for her trouble was a ripped shoulder seam. She gritted her teeth. 'Don't worry,' she muttered, clutching the drooping neckline with one hand and lifting the trailing hem with the other. 'I'm throwing this one out as soon as I get upstairs.'

His mouth curved at the corners, and he plucked a crushed flower petal from her tangled hair. 'Feel free to trash any others while you're at it. They won't be of

much use to you...not for long.' Before she could give
vent to her outrage, he instructed, 'Hurry up and get
dressed. I'm going to inspect the ranch this morning. I
leave in five minutes—with you...or without you.'

Leah didn't lose any time changing. Throwing on jeans
and a T-shirt, she stuffed her feet into boots. Securing
her hair into one long braid, she grabbed a hat from her
bedpost and raced downstairs. At some point she'd have
to move her things into the bedroom she now shared
with Hunter. But there would be plenty of opportunity
for that. Weeks. Months. She bit down on her lip. *Years*.

She found Hunter in the barn, saddling the horses.
He passed her a paper sack. 'Here. Thought you might
be hungry.'

'Thanks. I am.' Peeking inside, she found a half-dozen
of Inez's cinnamon and apple muffins. 'I don't suppose
you thought to bring coffee.'

'Thermos is in my saddlebag. Help yourself.' He
tightened the cinch on his buckskin and glanced at her.
'I moved that Appaloosa mare with the pulled tendon
to another stall. There's a leak at that end of the barn.
Looks like we'll need a new roof.'

She bit into a muffin. 'I'll have Patrick and a couple
of the men patch it,' she said, taking a quick gulp of
coffee.

'No.' He yanked the brim of his hat lower on his
forehead. 'I said the barn needs a new roof.'

She sighed, capping the Thermos and shoving it and
the sack of muffins back into his saddlebag. 'This is one
of those marital tests, isn't it?'

'Come again?'

'You know. A test. You say we need a new roof. I say
no we don't. You say, I'm the boss and we're getting a
new roof. And I say, but we can't afford a roof. And

you say, well, we're getting one anyway, even if we have to eat dirt for the next month to pay for it. And if I say anything further you start reminding me that before we married I promised this and I agreed to that, and that you're the boss and what you say goes. Does that about sum up what's happening here?'

He nodded, amusement lightening his expression. 'That about sums it up. Glad to see you catch on so fast.' He tossed her a bright yellow slicker. 'Here. Take this. Forecast calls for rain.'

'Hunter, we really can't afford a new roof.' She rolled the slicker and tied it to the back of her saddle. 'If we could, I'd have stuck one on last spring, or the spring before that, or even the spring before that.'

'We're getting a new roof.' He mounted. 'Though if it eases your mind any you won't have to eat dirt for the next month to pay for it.'

After a momentary hesitation she followed suit and climbed into the saddle. 'I won't?'

'Nope. Just for the next week.' He clicked his tongue, urging his horse into an easy trot.

They spent the morning investigating the eastern portion of the Hampton spread and Leah began to see the ranch through Hunter's eyes. And what she saw didn't please her. Signs of neglect were everywhere. Fence-lines sagged. Line-shacks had fallen into disrepair. A few of the cattle showed evidence of screwworm and the majority of the calves they came across hadn't been branded or vaccinated.

At the south-eastern tip of the range Hunter stopped by a small stream and dismounted. 'What the hell have your men been doing, Leah?' he asked, disgust heavy in his voice. 'There's no excuse for the condition of this place.'

'Money's been tight,' she protested defensively. 'We don't have a large work crew.'

'I've got news for you. You don't have a work crew, period. Leastwise they don't seem to be working worth a damn.'

'A lot of what we've seen isn't their fault, but mine,' she claimed, evading his searching stare. 'I haven't had the time recently to stay on top of everything.'

Hunter shook his head. 'Not good enough, Leah. Any foreman worth his salt would have caught most of these problems for you.'

'You told me you wouldn't fire anyone until they'd had an opportunity to prove themselves,' she said, taking a different tack. 'I know things look bad, but give us a chance. Tell us what you want done and we'll do it.'

He stripped off his gloves and tucked them in his belt. 'What I want is for you to get off that horse and sit down and discuss the situation with me. One way or another we're going to come to a meeting of the minds, and I can't think of a better time or place than right here and now.'

Still she resisted. 'If we sit under that pecan tree, we'll get ticks.'

He took off his hat and slapped the dust from the brim. 'Did you last time?'

So he did remember this spot. She'd wondered if his stopping here had been coincidental or deliberate. Now she knew. She closed her eyes. How much longer would she have to pay? she wondered in despair. When would it be enough? 'I might have found a tick or two,' she finally admitted.

'Then I'll look you over tonight,' he offered. 'Just to be on the safe side.'

'Thanks all the same,' she said drily. 'But I'll pass.'

He held out a hand. 'Let's go, Leah. I didn't bring you here to go skinny-dipping again. I brought you here to talk. We'll save a return trip down memory lane for another visit.'

Reluctantly, she dismounted. 'What do you want to discuss?'

'The repairs we need to make and your employees,' he stated succinctly.

'I vote we start with the repairs,' she said. 'Have you gotten the loan? Is that why you plan to replace the barn roof?'

'And fix up the line-shacks, and restring fence-line and increase the size of the herd. Yes, the loan's taken care of, and we have enough money to put the ranch back on its feet. But it isn't just lack of repairs that contribute to a ranch going downhill.'

She sank to the grass with a grimace, shifting to one side so he could join her. 'Time to discuss the employees?'

'Time to discuss the employees. I made a point of meeting most of them before we married.'

She gave him a direct look. 'Then you know why I hired them.'

'Leah——'

'Don't say another thing, Hunter! For once you're going to listen and I'm going to talk.' She fought to find the words to convince him, desperate to protect her workers. 'Not a single one of my employees has been able to find jobs anywhere else. The Arroyas were living out of a station wagon when I found them. Lenny's a veteran who doesn't care to sit around collecting government handouts. And Patrick risked his own life to save a child about to be run down by a drunk driver. He shattered his ankle doing it. A week later he got a pink slip because Lyon Enterprises didn't want to be bothered with an employee who might not be able to pull his own weight.'

Hunter shot her a sharp glance. 'He worked for Lyon Enterprises?'

'He used to be foreman of the Circle P. Bull Jones replaced him.'

'And you took Patrick in.'

'I've given them all a home,' she acknowledged. 'I've given them a life. And, as a result, they earn a living. More importantly, they've regained their self-respect. So their work isn't always perfect. I can assure you that it's the best they're capable of doing. But if you ask for more they'll do everything in their power to give it to you. That's how much working here means to them. They're family. Don't ask me to turn my back on family, because I can't do it.'

He stared out across the pastureland. 'You always were a sucker for an underdog. I often thought that was what attracted you to me.'

'That's not true.' She stopped, afraid of revealing too much. She'd never seen him as an underdog. A champion, a man of drive and determination, someone filled with an intense passion and strength. But not once had she ever seen him as an underdog.

His mouth tightened, as though he'd mistakenly allowed her to get too close—revealed too much of himself. 'That still doesn't change the facts. And the facts are that you can't run a ranch without competent help.'

'Hunter,' she pleaded. 'Give them a fair chance. No more, no less. I swear I won't ask you for anything else.'

His expression turned skeptical. 'Won't you?'

'No. I won't. Because saving the ranch isn't worth it to me if I can't save them as well.'

That caught his attention. 'You'd give up the ranch if it came to a choice between running at a profit or replacing the help?'

She considered his question at length, a frown creasing her brow. 'I suspect I would,' she admitted at last. 'Because otherwise I'd be no better than Lyon Enterprises. And if I wanted to be like them, I'd have sold out long ago.'

'You're that serious about it?'

She nodded. 'I'm that serious.'

It was his turn to consider. Slowly he nodded. 'Okay. We'll do it your way. For now. But I can't make any guarantees about the future. Will that do?'

'I guess it'll have to,' she said with a shrug.

'Why don't we swing south next, and inspect that side of the ranch? Then we'll call it a day.'

'I'm ready,' she claimed, happy to agree now that she'd been granted a reprieve. 'Let's go.'

He shook his head. 'Not yet. There's just one more thing I want before we head out. And I want it from you.'

'What?' she asked warily, his tone warning her that she wouldn't like his request.

'I want you to kiss me.'

'What?' she repeated in a fainter voice.

'You heard me. I want a kiss. I'm willing to wait until you're ready before we go any further, but there's no reason we can't enjoy a preview of coming attractions.' He held her with a searing gaze. 'Come on, Leah. It's not a lot to ask.'

It wasn't, and she knew it. Not giving herself a chance to reconsider, she leaned closer, resting her hands on his chest. She stared up at him, at the features that were almost as familiar as her own. The changes time had wrought were few, more of a strengthening, a fulfillment of what was once a promise. The lines furrowing his brow and radiating from the corners of his eyes reflected a deepening of character that had come with age and experience.

Tenderly she cupped his face, exploring anew the taut, high-boned planes of his cheeks. It had been so long, so very long. Slowly, she allowed her fingers to sink into his thick black hair and, tilting her head just slightly, she feathered a soft, teasing kiss across his mouth. She half expected him to grab her, to crush her in his arms and take what he so clearly wanted. But he didn't. He remained perfectly still, allowing her to set the pace.

She continued to tease, dropping tiny kisses across his jaw and neck before returning to explore his lips. And then she kissed him, really kissed him, the way a woman kissed her man. And for the first time he responded, not with his hands and arms, but with his mouth alone, returning her urgent, eager caresses with a mind-drugging thoroughness that left her shaken and defenseless. He had to know how she felt—had to be aware of how much she gave away with that kiss, how her protective barrier lay in total ruin. At long last his arms closed around her, enfolding her in the sweetest of embraces, and she knew in that moment that she'd willingly give him anything he asked.

How much time passed, Leah wasn't sure. One minute she existed in a sensual haze, secure in his arms, the next Hunter thrust her from him, tumbling her to the ground. In a move so swift that she barely registered it he spun around, crouching protectively in front of her. To her horror, a wickedly curved knife appeared in his hand.

'You're trespassing, Jones. What's your business here?' Hunter demanded.

It wasn't until then that Leah noticed the foreman of the Circle P, mounted on a bay, not more than fifteen feet away. She hadn't heard his approach. But Hunter had.

'Tell your guard-dog to drop the knife, Leah,' Bull Jones called, his gaze riveted to the glinting length of steel in Hunter's hand. 'Or I'll have to get serious with some buckshot.' His hand inched toward his rifle. 'You *comprende* what I'm saying, *hombre*? You have no business threatening me. I'd only be defending myself if I was forced to shoot.'

The expression in Hunter's eyes burned with unmistakable menace. 'You'll feel the hurting end of this blade long before that Remington clears your scabbard. You *comprende* me, *muchacho*? Play it smart. Ride out now.'

For a minute Leah feared that Bull would pull his gun. His hand wavered over the rifle butt for an endless moment, before settling on his thigh. 'Since you're new to the Hampton spread I'll cut you some slack,' he addressed Hunter. 'But nobody threatens me. Ever. Somebody'd better explain that to you pronto, because next time I won't let you off so easy.'

'Last warning.' The blade quivered in Hunter's hand. 'Ride. Now.'

'You'll regret this, Leah,' Bull hollered. Swearing beneath his breath, he sawed at his mount's bit and rode off.

'Oh, God,' Leah moaned, and she began to tremble. In one supple move, Hunter sheathed his knife in his boot and pulled her into his arms.

'It's okay,' he murmured against the top of her head. 'He's gone.'

She clung to him, unable to stop shaking, reaction setting in fast and hard. He didn't release her, just stood silently, enveloping her in a tight, inviolable hold. Yet she'd have had him hold her closer if she thought her ribs would stand the strain. Slowly the warmth of his body and the strength of his arms calmed her, soothing her terror.

'He could have shot you,' she whispered, fighting to hold back her tears.

He tucked a strand of hair behind her ear. 'Not a chance. I had him dead to rights and he knew it.' His mouth brushed her cheek, her jaw, her lips. 'It's over, Leah. He's gone.'

She melted against him, needing his touch more desperately than she'd ever needed anything before in her life. As though sensing it, he kissed her. But it wasn't like the passionate embrace they'd shared earlier. This caress was so gentle and tender that it nearly broke her heart.

'He frightens me, Hunter,' she confessed in a low voice.

He glanced at the thin cloud of dust disappearing to the south. 'Tell me about him.' It was an order.

She fought to gather her thoughts enough to give him a coherent answer. 'I've told you most of it. Although I can't prove anything, I suspect he's responsible for our fence-lines being cut. We've had a couple of suspicious stampedes and one or two of the wells have been fouled.' She shrugged. 'That sort of thing.'

'He's the reason this place is so neglected.' It wasn't a question. 'You don't ride out here alone, do you? That's why you haven't seen the problems until now.'

She bowed her head. 'I don't let the others come either,' she admitted. 'Unless they're in a group. I've been terrified of something happening.'

'Have you reported any of this to Lyon Enterprises?'

She flashed him a bitter glare. 'Who do you think he's getting his instructions from?'

'Do you know that for a fact?'

She whirled free of his arms, anger replacing her fear. 'I don't know anything for a fact. If I did, Bull Jones would be in jail and I'd have a nice, fat lawsuit pending against Lyon Enterprises. You married me to get your hands on this ranch, didn't you? If you want to keep it, you're going to have to defend it. Otherwise we both lose.'

Hunter bent down and retrieved his hat. 'Mount up.'

She stared in disbelief. 'Now? Just like that? End of discussion?'

'I want to check the south pasture before dark.'

'That's the direction Bull took. What if we run into him again?' she asked nervously.

The brim of his hat threw Hunter's face into shadow, making his expression unreadable. 'Then I'll make a point of introducing myself.'

She clung to him, checking his move toward his horse. 'Please, Hunter. Can't we go home? We can check the south pasture tomorrow. There's no point in looking for trouble.'

A humorless smile cut across his face. 'You've got it backward. Seems trouble has come looking for us.' For a minute she thought he'd insist they explore the south pasture. But at long last he nodded. 'Okay. I've seen enough. But tomorrow I ride south.' And with that she had to be satisfied.

In the study, Hunter lifted the phone receiver and stared at it for a long minute before punching in a series of numbers. After several clicks the call was connected.

'Kevin Anderson.'

'It's Hunter. Give me an update.' He listened to the lengthy recitation with a frown and jotted down a few notes. 'Okay. Don't do anything for now. We don't want to tip our hand. The rest can wait until I come in.'

'Any problems at your end?' Kevin asked.

'You might say that.' Hunter poured himself a shot of whiskey, and downed it in a single swallow. 'I had another run-in with Bull Jones.'

Alarm sounded in Kevin's voice. 'Does he know who you are yet?'

'Not yet. Our marriage has been kept pretty much under wraps. Not a lot of people know. But Jones could be a problem once he finds out—depending on how much talking he decides to do.'

'What do you want me to do?'

'Send me his file. Overnight it.'

'Will do. Then what? You want him...out of the picture?'

Hunter thought about it, rubbing a weary hand across the back of his neck. 'No. Don't do anything for now. We act too soon and it'll give the whole game away.'

'Whatever you say. You're the boss.'

'Thanks, Kevin.'

Hanging up, Hunter poured a final shot of whiskey and stared at the ceiling. Time to bed down with his beautiful bride. Time to pull that soft, sweet piece of feminine delight into his arms and...sleep. He downed the liquor, praying that it would numb him—at least the parts in dire need of numbing. Patience. He only needed a little more patience. And then that soft, sweet piece of feminine delight would be all his.

CHAPTER SIX

LEAH slipped from Hunter's arms at the crack of dawn the next morning. This time she kept yesterday's warning firmly in mind, and dressed before going to the kitchen for an apple. Running to the south pasture fence, she whistled for her stallion. But instead of the horse all she found was a white-tailed deer and a family of jack-rabbits who, startled by her sudden appearance, burst across the grassland and disappeared from view. She climbed on to the top rail and waited for a while, but Dreamseeker proved surprisingly elusive.

Concluding that she'd been stood up in favor of a patch of fresh clover, she bit into the apple. Then she watched as the sun gathered strength, spreading its warm April rays across a nearby field splattered with the vivid purple of bluebonnets and neon-orange of Indian paint-brush. Without question this had to be her favorite time of the day—as well as her favorite season of the year.

A twig snapped behind her. 'Beautiful, isn't it?' she asked in a conversational tone of voice.

'Yes.' Hunter folded his arms across the top rail and glanced at her. 'No accusations of sneaking up on you this morning?'

'You banged the kitchen door.'

'And stomped across the yard.'

A tiny grin touched her mouth. 'I almost turned around to look, but you were being so considerate that I didn't want to spoil it.'

'I appreciate your restraint,' he said, with a touch of wry humor. 'Your horse hasn't shown up yet?'

She frowned, tossing her apple core into the meadow. 'He didn't answer my whistle. But if we're exploring the south pasture we're bound to come across him. Ready to go?' She vaulted off the fence, wanting to get Hunter's inspection tour over and done with. Perhaps if they made an early start they'd avoid Bull Jones.

'No. I'm not ready.' He caught her arm, tugging her to a standstill. 'Not quite yet.'

'Why?' she asked in apprehension. 'Is there something wrong?'

'You might say that.' His hold lightened, though he didn't release her. 'You were gone again this morning.'

She bridled at the hint of censure in his voice. She'd agreed to sleep with him without too much argument; surely he didn't intend to choose which hours that would encompass. If so, he'd soon learn differently. 'Is that a problem?'

'Yes. I don't like it. Tomorrow you start the day in my arms.'

She eased from his grip and a took a quick step back, something in his expression filling her with a discomfiting awareness. 'What difference does it make if I'm there or not?' she asked.

Her question seemed to amuse him. 'If you wake me tomorrow, you'll learn the difference.'

She didn't doubt it for a minute. But that didn't mean she'd go along. 'I'll consider it,' she conceded. 'But I like having mornings to myself.'

'You'll have other times to yourself,' he informed her. 'I want time alone with you. All marriages need privacy...intimacy.'

Understanding dawned and she fought to breathe normally. So the moment of truth had finally arrived. If she read his request correctly, tomorrow morning she'd fulfill her duties as his wife and make their marriage a real, fully functioning union—no matter how much she wanted to resist. No matter how much that final act alarmed her. That was what she'd committed herself to when they'd exchanged their vows, and that was what she'd soon have to face. If only the thought didn't fill her with dread—dread that she'd couldn't keep a small part of herself safe from his possession; dread that when he took her body he'd take her heart as well.

'All right,' she said at last. 'Mornings can be our time.'

He inclined his head. 'We'll discuss the afternoons and evenings later.'

'Hunter——'

'Time to get to work.' He cut her off, amusement gleaming in his dark eyes. 'Are there any more of those muffins we had yesterday?'

'Plenty,' she admitted grudgingly. 'Inez left us well-stocked. I'll go get them.'

'And a Thermos of coffee, if you would. I'll saddle the horses.'

Fifteen minutes later they rode out, heading south along the fence-line. Hunter's buckskin seemed particularly agitated, fighting the bit and shying at the least little movement. Not that he had any trouble controlling the animal, but Leah could tell that their battle of wills wasn't the norm. As though in response, her mare fidgeted as well.

'Is it something in the air?' she asked uneasily. 'Lady-finger never acts up like this.'

'Something has them spooked,' he agreed. 'Have your men noticed any sign of cougar recently?'

'None.' She felt a sudden stabbing concern for Dreamseeker. 'It wasn't that hard a winter. There's no reason for one to come this close when the pickings are so easy further out.' But she knew her protests were more to convince herself than to convince him.

'Don't panic. I didn't say it was a cougar. I just thought we should consider the possibility.' He regarded her intently. 'I want you to stay alert, you got me? In the meantime, we have fence-line to inspect. So, let's get to it.'

They didn't converse much after that. Leah kept an eye open for anything out of the ordinary. And, though the animals remained skittish, she couldn't determine what caused their strange behavior.

A short time later Hunter stopped to examine a drooping length of barbed wire. 'This next section abuts Lyon Enterprises' property, doesn't it?' he asked, clearly annoyed with the condition of the fence.

'From here onward,' she confirmed.

'You're just asking for trouble, letting it fall into such a state of disrepair. One good shove and you'll have a week's worth of work combing Circle P hills for your herd. It gets top priority come Monday morning.'

'What about Bull Jones?' she asked uneasily.

A muscle tightened in his jaw. 'You let me worry about him. I don't expect it'll take long to reach an understanding.'

By noon they'd almost finished their inspection. Riding over a low hill, they suddenly discovered the reason for their horses' agitation. The fence between the two ranches lay on the ground. And down a steep grade, on Lyon property, grazed Dreamseeker...with the Circle P mare he'd corralled.

Hunter reined to a stop and shot Leah a sharp look. 'He's a stallion? That horse you were with yesterday morning?'

She glanced at him in surprise. 'Didn't you notice?'

'No, I didn't notice,' came the blunt retort. 'Because it wasn't the damned horse that caught my eye.'

Then what...? Realization swiftly dawned, and color mounted her cheeks. Not what. Who. He'd been distracted by her...and the fact that she'd only been wearing a nightgown. Well, she couldn't help that. Nor did it change anything. 'I don't see what difference it makes whether or not he's a stallion——'

'There's a big difference,' he cut her off. 'Not many geldings I know are going to bust through a fence to get to a mare in heat. But you can count on a stallion doing it every time.' He shoved his hat to the back of his head, apparently debating his options.

Leah didn't show any such hesitation. As far as she was concerned, only one option existed. Without giving thought to the consequences, she charged across the smashed fence and started after her stallion. Or she would have, if Hunter hadn't been quite so quick. He spurred his horse into action and blocked her path.

'What the hell do you think you're doing?' he shouted, grabbing her horse's bridle and jerking her to a stop.

As much as she wanted to fight his hold, she didn't dare risk injuring Ladyfinger's delicate mouth. 'What does it look like I'm doing?' she flashed back. 'I'm getting my horse. Let go, Hunter. We don't have much time.'

He stared in disbelief. 'You can't be serious.'

'I'm very serious.' Responding to her agitation, Ladyfinger attempted to rear, but a soft word and a gentle hand brought her under control. Leah spoke urgently. 'If Bull Jones finds Dreamseeker on his property, he'll shoot first and ask questions later. I have to get my horse out of there before that happens.' She gathered up the reins, prepared to rip free at the first opportunity.

As though he sensed her intentions, his hold tightened on Ladyfinger's bridle, preventing any sudden movement on her part. 'You try and rope that animal and he'll kill you—which won't matter because I'll have killed you long before he has the chance.'

'Hunter,' she interrupted, prepared to dismount and go after Dreamseeker on foot, 'we're wasting precious time.'

'Tough. You have two choices,' he informed her. 'You can keep fighting me in which case that stallion will stay down there until hell freezes over. Or...'

'Or?' she prompted impatiently.

'Or you can do exactly what I say and we might get him out of there. But I'm telling you, Leah. You ever do anything as stupid as coming between a stallion and his mare and I won't be responsible for my actions.'

'Not responsible...' Anger flared and she made no attempt to curb it. 'That's what you said about my running around in my nightgown! That's a pretty broad range you've got going there. Maybe you'd better tell me what other actions alleviate you of your responsibilities. Just so there won't be any doubt in my mind.'

'Believe me, the second you commit one, you'll be the first to know.'

She didn't miss the implication. He'd let her know in his own distinctive manner—and chances were excellent that it would involve another of those mind-splintering kisses. She opened her mouth to argue, and was instantly cut off.

'Well? What's it going to be? My way or no way.'

More than anything she wanted to tell him to go to hell. But one quick glance at Dreamseeker and she knew she didn't have any other choice. 'Your way,' she gave in grudgingly. 'How hard will it be to get him back?'

'That depends on how long he's been down there with that mare. With any luck it's been all morning, and he's expended most of his...enthusiasm.'

She eyed the seemingly placid animal. 'By the look of him I'd say he's expended plenty of enthusiasm.'

Hunter didn't appear as certain. 'We'll see. Tie Ladyfinger out of the way and stand by the fence. I'm going to rope the mare and try and bring her across. Dreamseeker will give chase. The second they're both on our property, you get that fence-line back up. If anything goes wrong, stand clear and *don't interfere.*' Serious dark eyes held her with an implacable gaze. 'Got it?'

'Got it.' Following his instructions, she tied her horse out of the way and stuck her fence tool and staples into her utility belt. Pulling on work-gloves, she took up a stance by the downed lines and gave him a nod. 'Ready when you are.'

Jamming his hat low on his brow, he released his rope and slowly rode down the hill. He waited near the bottom. Not wanting to arouse Dreamseeker's territorial instincts, he kept his distance from the mare, and though Leah could barely contain her impatience she knew that Hunter hoped the stallion would make things easy and move off a ways, allowing for a clear shot at the mare. Everything considered, the throw would be a difficult one.

Ten long minutes ticked by before an opportunity presented itself. Gently, he swung the rope overhead and tossed. Leah held her breath as it soared through the air...and landed directly on target. With a swiftness born of both experience and a strong desire to get the deed done before Dreamseeker caught wind of his intentions, Hunter dallied the rope around the horn and began to pull the mare up the hill.

The trapped animal fought him, rearing and pawing the air. Dragging a horse in the exact opposite direction from where she wanted to go was bad enough, but having to do it up a hill made it near impossible. Leah could hear Hunter swearing beneath his breath, the sound of his saddle creaking and his horse blowing carrying to her as they inched their way toward Hampton property.

About halfway up the hill Dreamseeker suddenly realized what they were about. With a shriek of outrage, the stallion gave chase. Hunter's buckskin didn't need any more encouragement than that. The sight of seventeen hundred pounds of rampaging stallion barreling straight for them apparently inspired the gelding to redouble his efforts. Even the mare seemed to lose her reluctance.

All too quickly Dreamseeker reached them. Instead of attacking Hunter, the stallion nipped at the mare, who stopped fighting the rope and abruptly changed direction, charging up the hill, the stallion on her heels. It was all Hunter could do to get out of the way.

'Leah, stand clear!' he shouted.

Intent on regaining his own territory, Dreamseeker drove the frightened mare before him up the hill and on to Hampton property. As the horses stormed past Hunter released the rope and followed close behind.

'Get that fence up fast, before he changes his mind,' Hunter bellowed over his shoulder, positioning himself between Leah and the threatening stallion. An agitated Dreamseeker milled nearby, clearly uncertain whether to challenge the intruders or escape with his prize. Hunter tensed, prepared for either eventuality.

Not wasting a single second, Leah slammed staples into the post, securing the barbed wire. Not that it would stop Dreamseeker if he decided to head back to the Circle P. But maybe now that he'd successfully captured a mare and returned to his own domain he'd be less inclined to break through again. She cast an uneasy glance at her horse. At least, he wouldn't break through unless there were more mares to be had.

With a shrill whinny, Dreamseeker finally chose to retreat. Racing away from them, he hustled the mare
toward the far side of the pasture. Assured that the
danger had passed, Hunter climbed off his buckskin and
tied him to the fence.

'Where's Ladyfinger?' he asked, freeing his fence tool
from its holster.

She spared him a quick look. 'Broke the reins and
took off. I guess she figured that Dreamseeker meant
business and didn't want to get between him and
whatever that business might be.'

He made a sound of impatience. 'You'll have to ride
with me. Once we're done here, we'll head on in.'

'Right.' She didn't dare say more, not until he'd had
a chance to cool off. He joined her at the fence, helping
to string wire and reinforce the posts. They worked side
by side for several minutes before Leah thought to ask,
'What do we do about that mare?'

'We aren't going to do anything. When she isn't such
a bone of contention I'll cut her loose and return her to
the Circle P.'

Leah paused in her efforts. 'What about Bull Jones?'

To her surprise a slight smile touched Hunter's mouth.
'I'll send him a bill for stud service.' He strung the final
line of wire and glanced at her. 'Is that stallion saddle-
broken?'

She shook her head. 'Not yet, but——'

'He's wild?' Hunter didn't wait for her confirmation.
'He goes.'

She straightened, wiping perspiration from her brow.
'You can't be serious!'

'I'm dead serious. He's dangerous and I won't risk
your safety on a dangerous animal.'

'Then you'll have to get rid of the bulls, the cows and
every other critter around here,' she retorted in exas-

peration. 'Because in the right circumstances any one of them could be considered dangerous, too.'

'I'm not changing my mind,' he stated unequivocally, stamping the ground around a listing post.

How could she explain Dreamseeker's importance? Hunter would never understand. She wasn't sure she understood. All she knew was that the stallion touched a need, fulfilled a fantasy of being unfettered and without responsibilities. Though part of her hoped some day to tame the wild beast, another part longed to allow the stallion his freedom—just as she longed to experience a similar freedom. It was an unrealistic dream, but she didn't care.

Looking Hunter straight in the eye, Leah said, 'Don't do it. Please don't get rid of him. He means the world to me.'

His expression turned grim and remote. 'Another hard luck case?'

'In a way,' she admitted. 'I took him in when others might have put him down. I suspect he's been abused in the past, which would explain his skittishness.'

Hunter leaned his forearms across the post, his plaid shirt pulled tight across his broad chest. A fine sheen of perspiration glinted in the hollow of his throat, and his thick ebony hair clung to his brow—a brow furrowed in displeasure. 'You're doing a poor job persuading me to let him stay. If anything, you've convinced me he's too dangerous. Besides, you used up all your favors yesterday, remember?'

'I remember.' Having him give her employees a chance was still more important to her than any other consideration—even saving Dreamseeker. 'I'm not asking for another favor. I promised I wouldn't, and I won't.' She offered a crooked smile. 'But I'm willing to compromise.'

'You're pushing it.'

She nodded. 'I know. But it's important to me.'

He frowned, and she could sense his struggle between what common sense told him to do and granting her plea. Finally he nodded. 'One month. If I can break him, or at least put some manners on him, he can stay. But you keep clear in the meantime. Agreed?'

Her smile widened. 'Agreed.'

'That's the last time, Leah,' he warned. 'You've pushed me to the limit. Now, mount up.'

'My horse...?' she reminded him.

'I haven't forgotten. We'll ride double.'

He crossed to his buckskin and untied the reins from the fence. Looking from Hunter to the horse, Leah caught her breath in dismay. With her clinging to his back like a limpet, dipping and swaying, rubbing and bumping all the way to the ranch, it would be a long ride home. She shivered.

Real long.

Leah began to ease from the bed the next day, as she had each of the other two mornings, but then remembered her promise to stay. With a tiny sigh she lay down again, and yanked the sheet to her chin. Instantly Hunter caught hold of her, ripped the sheet free and tumbled her into a warm embrace.

'Good morning, wife,' he muttered close to her ear.

'Good morning,' she responded cautiously, waiting for him to pounce, to force himself on her. Considering her forty-eight-hour deadline had expired last night, he'd be well within his rights. Instead he enclosed her hair in a possessive fist and, dropping an arm across her waist, shut his eyes. His breathing deepened and she frowned. 'The sun's up,' she prompted, fighting nervous anticipation.

'Uh-huh.'

He nuzzled her cheek and she drew back. 'This is our time together, remember?'

'I remember.'

'Well?' She could hear the strain in her voice, but couldn't help it. She wanted to get whatever he had planned over and done with. 'You said this time together would make a difference. The only difference I've noticed is that I'm late starting my chores.'

He sighed, opening one eye. 'The chores can wait. Relax. You're stiff as a board.' He slid an arm around her hips and tucked her back against his chest, spoon-fashion. Resting his chin on top of her head, he said, 'Now just relax and talk to me.'

'Talk.' This wasn't quite what she'd expected when he'd made his demand. She'd suspected that he intended to...to do a whole lot more than talk. 'What should I talk about?'

'Anything. Everything. Whatever comes to mind.'

'Okay,' she agreed, knowing she sounded stilted and uncomfortable. 'What are your plans for this morning?'

'I'll start by working with Dreamseeker.'

'And...and the fence-line? The one that runs alongside of the Circle P?'

'It gets fixed today.'

'You'll be careful?' She hesitated to mention her fears, but couldn't help herself. 'I don't trust Bull.'

'I'll take care of it.'

'It's just——' He brushed a length of hair from her brow and she realized that at some point during their conversation she'd rolled over to face him. And with the realization her words died away, and her earlier nervousness returned.

He noticed. She suspected that his sharp, black-eyed gaze noticed everything. Gently, he cupped her cheek, his callused thumb stroking the corner of her mouth.

'I'll take care of it,' he repeated, and kissed her warmly, deeply, sparking an instant response.

She didn't reply—couldn't, in fact. He seemed to sense that, for he pressed his advantage, his kiss becoming more intense, more urgent. Sensing her capitulation, he pressed her into the mattress. Instantly her body reacted, softening as his hardened, moving in concert with his, shifting to accommodate his size and weight.

Her nightgown provided no barrier at all. He unbuttoned the small pearl buttons that ran from neck to waist and swept the cotton from her shoulders. Drawing back, he gazed down at her, the early morning light playing across the taut, drawn lines of his face. Kneeling above her, he seemed like some bold conqueror of old, a bronzed warrior poised to take what he willed, and giving no quarter. Slowly, he reached for her, his black eyes burning like twin flames. His fists closed around her nightgown, and in one swift move he stripped it from her.

Reacting instinctively, she fought to cover herself, the expression on his face frightening her. She shouldn't struggle. She knew she shouldn't, but sudden blind panic overrode all other thought and emotion.

'No!' The tiny urgent whisper escaped before she could prevent it.

'Don't fight me,' he demanded, trapping her beneath him and staring down with intense, passion-filled eyes. 'I won't hurt you. Dammit, Leah! You know how good it was between us, how good it can be again.'

'I know, I know,' she moaned, a sob catching in her throat. 'I can't help it. It's not the same any more. I can't make myself feel what I did before just because we're married now...just because it's what you want.'

'And you don't?' he bit out. His hand swept across the rigid peak of her breast. 'You're only fooling yourself if that's what you think. You can't deny your body's response to me.'

'No, I can't.' The confession, raw and painful, was torn from her. How she wished she could open herself to his embrace and enjoy the momentary pleasure he offered, regardless of the consequences. But something instinctively held her back, making the gesture impossible. He'd taken so much already. She didn't dare allow him to take more. Not yet.

'Give yourself to me, Leah.' His words were raspy, heavy with desire. 'You want to. Stop resisting.'

Urgently, she shook her head. 'I won't be a pawn in your game of revenge. You have the ranch. You can't have me. Not this easily. And not with such casual disregard.'

'You call this casual?' He gripped her hand, drawing it to his body, encouraging the hesitant stroke of her fingers against his heated skin. 'Touch me and then try and call what I feel casual.'

Unable to resist, her hand followed the sinewy contours from chest to abdomen. 'If you feel something, then say the words,' she pleaded. 'Tell me our love-making isn't just sex. Tell me honestly that there isn't some deep, secret part of you settling an old score.' Tears filled her eyes. 'Tell me that, Hunter, so I don't feel used.'

He tensed above her, his hands tightening on her shoulders in automatic reaction. Then his head dropped to her breast, a day's growth of whiskers rasping across her skin, branding her. A tear escaped from the corner of her eye. She had her answer. She'd gambled and lost. His very silence condemned him, told her more clearly than any words that his motivations were far from pure, that his actions weren't inspired by anything as noble as love.

'I could take you by force.' His voice was raw and harsh against her breast.

She prayed that it was only frustration speaking, that his threat was an empty one. 'You once told me force wouldn't be necessary. Have you changed your mind?' She attempted to slip from beneath him, but his hands closed around her shoulders, holding her in place. 'Taking what you want won't help our situation any,' she tried to reason with him.

'The hell it won't! It would help my situation a great deal. And I'd bet my last dollar that it would do a world of good for yours.'

She couldn't deny the truth. She turned her face into the pillow, retreating from the accusation in his eyes. Helpless tears escaped despite her attempts to control them. 'I'm sorry. I wish I could give myself to you and be done with it. But I can't. I can't be that detached about making love.'

'I don't expect you to be detached. I do expect you to resign yourself to the inevitable and face facts.' He threaded his fingers through her hair, forcing her to face him. 'And the fact is, we will be lovers. It will happen whether it's tomorrow or the next day or the one after that. Before long, wife, you'll want my touch. I guarantee it.'

'You're wrong,' she insisted, but they both knew she lied.

With an unexpectedly calming hand he brushed the tears from her cheeks. 'I won't force the issue this time. But understand me; I don't make any promises for the next.'

Then he rolled off her and left the bed... left Leah to her thoughts and to the inescapable knowledge that resisting him would prove futile. Soon her body would betray her and she'd be unable to stop him from completing what he'd started today. And once that happened, he'd have won it all.

Leah headed for the corral a short time later, to observe Hunter work with Dreamseeker. She wasn't alone. The Arroya children and a number of the employees all found excuses to line up along the fence and watch the coming confrontation. But if they had thought that Hunter would simply climb on to the stallion's back and attempt to bust him, they were mistaken. Instead, he lifted a piece of saddle-blanket from the corral fence and, after letting the horse sniff it, ran it over Dreamseeker's shoulders.

'Easy, boy. Easy.' His deep voice carried on the early morning breeze as he calmed the nervous animal.

Leah watched his hands and listened to his low reassurances, uncomfortably aware that his gentling of the nervous animal was remarkably similar to the way he'd soothed her before leaving their bed. She didn't doubt for a minute who would win this battle of wills... any more than she doubted who would ultimately win the age-old battle waged in their bedroom. It was as inevitable as the changing of the seasons; time was the only variable.

Once done with Dreamseeker, he spent until sundown laboring with the men, starting to set the ranch to rights.

As the days winged by, Leah began to relax. He didn't press her to commit to him physically and, contrary to her earlier fears, he also didn't make any sweeping changes. Instead he did just as he'd promised. He gave her employees a chance.

Or so she thought until Inez came tearing up to the corral fence.

'Señora, come quick! The men, they are fighting.'

Leah leapt from the horse she'd been training and ducked beneath the fence-rails. 'Where?'

'Behind the barn.'

She ran flat out, skidding to a stop as she came around the corner of the barn. Sprawled in the dust lay one of her more recent hard luck cases; a huge, brawny youngster barely past his teens by the name of Orrie. Above him towered Hunter, his fists cocked, his stance threatening. The rest of the employees stood in a loose circle around the two.

'Hunter!' she called, horrified that he'd actually fight one of her workers, especially one so young.

He spared her a brief glance. 'Stay out of it, Leah,' he warned. 'This doesn't concern you.'

Orrie scrambled to his feet, careful to keep clear of Hunter's reach. 'He fired me, Miz Hampton. He had no call to do that. You have to help me.'

Uncertain, she looked from Orrie to her husband. 'What's this about?'

Hunter's mouth tightened. 'You heard me, Leah. Stay out of it.'

'You have to do something, Miz Hampton,' Orrie insisted, bolting to her side. 'You can't let him get away with it. He's trying to change things.'

'You must be mistaken. He promised to give everyone a fair shot,' she hastened to reassure. 'Do your job and you stay.' She searched the sea of faces for confirmation. 'That was the agreement, right?'

Bitterness filled Orrie's expression. 'Then he strung you along with his lies as well as the rest of us, 'cause he fired me. And that ain't all!' The words were tumbling from him, as though he feared being stopped. Forcibly. 'Lenny's gonna have to leave, too. And he's made Mateo give up the horses.'

She couldn't hide her disbelief. 'Hunter, you can't do that!'

'I can and I have.' He motioned to the men. 'You have your orders. Get to it.' Without a word, they drifted away from the scene.

Orrie stared at her with the saddest, most pathetic eyes she'd ever seen. 'You won't let him fire me, will you, Miz Hampton?'

'Her name is Pryde. *Mrs* Pryde,' Hunter stated coldly. He snagged his hat from the dirt and slapped the dust from the brim. 'And she has no say in this. You have your wages, which is more than you deserve. Pick up your bedroll and clear out.' He started toward them. 'Now.'

Orrie hesitated, shifting so that Leah stood between him and trouble. 'Miz Hampton...Pryde?'

She switched her attention from her employee to Hunter. 'Perhaps if I understood the reason?' she suggested, hoping he'd take the hint and explain himself.

Instead he folded his arms across his chest. 'There's nothing to understand. This is between me and the boy. I suggest you go to the house.'

She stared in shock. 'What?'

'You heard me. You're interfering. So, say goodbye to your friend here and get up to the house. Believe me. I'll be right behind.'

It sounded more like a threat than a promise. For a long minute she stood glaring at him, too furious to speak and too uncertain of the possible consequences to stand her ground. With a muffled exclamation, she turned and walked away, knowing that her cheeks burned with outrage. She could only pray that none of her other employees had been close enough to witness their battle of wills. Especially when she'd been so thoroughly defeated.

'Miz Hampton,' Orrie cried, dogging her retreat. 'Please. You gotta do something.'

She paused, glancing at him apologetically. 'It's out of my hands,' she admitted, risking a quick nervous look over her shoulder.

'That's it? You're going to let him fire me? You're going to give in to that... that half-breed?'

She pulled away in distaste. 'Don't *ever* use that expression around me.'

He'd made a mistake, and apparently knew it. He hastened to correct the situation. 'I... I didn't mean to say that,' he apologized. 'You gotta understand. I'm desperate. I have nowhere else to go.'

It took all her willpower to resist his pleas. 'I'm sorry. There's nothing I can do,' she said, and continued walking.

She didn't turn around again. Once at the house, she stormed into the study and stood helplessly by the window, watching Orrie's departure. Hunter watched too, remaining dead center in the middle of the drive while the youngster packed his things into Patrick's pick-up and finally left. Then Hunter turned and faced the house, grim intent marking every line of his body.

Leah didn't even realize that she'd backed from the window until she found herself up against her father's desk. Not taking time to analyze her reasons, she put the width of the oak tabletop between her and the study door. A minute later it crashed open.

Hunter strode in, slamming the door behind him so hard that it rocked on its hinges. 'You and I,' he announced in a furious voice, 'have a small matter to set straight.'

CHAPTER SEVEN

'YOU'RE angry,' she said, stating the obvious...stating the *very* obvious.

He started across the room. 'Good guess.'

'Well, I'm angry too.' She swallowed hard. 'I suggest we discuss this.'

He kept coming.

'Calmly.'

He knocked a mahogany hat rack from his path.

'Rationally.'

He stalked around the desk.

'Like two civilized adults.' She retreated, using her father's swivel chair as a shield. 'Okay?'

In response, he kicked the chair out of the way and trapped her against the wall.

'That's a yes, right?' she said with a gasp.

A muscle jerked in his cheek and he made a small growling sound low in his throat that told her more clearly than anything else just how furious he was. It took every ounce of willpower not to panic and bolt from the room. He grabbed her wrist in one hand and yanked. Bending low, he clipped her across the hips and tossed her over his shoulder.

'*Hunter*! No, don't!' she had time to shriek, before her entire world turned upside-down.

He clamped an arm around her legs just above the knees, effectively immobilizing her. 'We're going to discuss this all right. But not here where everyone and her grandmother can listen in,' he announced.

'Put me down!' She planted her palms in the middle of his back and attempted to wiggle free. Not that it did any good. His grip was as strong as a steel band.

'We could continue this conversation at the line-shack, if you'd prefer.' He shrugged his shoulders, bouncing her like a sack of potatoes. The breath whooshed from her lungs and she stopped bucking.

'No! Why not here? The study is an excellent place for a discussion. You start discussing and you'll see how good a place it is.'

'I say it's not.'

He'd reached the door and Leah began to panic seriously. 'Hunter, please. Put me down.'

He ignored her, stepping into the hallway. Heading for the entrance, he tipped his hat and said, 'Afternoon, Rose. Glad you could drop in. Or should I say eavesdrop in? My bride and I are going for a little drive.'

'You don't say.' Rose folded her arms across her chest. 'You're going to have trouble driving like that.'

'It's amazing the things you can accomplish when you set your mind to it. Don't wait dinner for us.' With that, he left the house. Beside his pick-up, he dropped Leah to her feet, and held the truck door open. 'Your choice. You can get in under your own steam, or I can help you.'

She planted her hands on her hips. 'I am perfectly capable of getting into a truck all on my own, thank you very much.'

'Wrong answer.' The next thing she knew, he'd scooped her up and dumped her on the passenger seat. Slamming the door closed, he leaned in the window. 'This conversation may take longer than I thought. Stay here.'

Before she could say a single word, he'd started off toward the barn. He returned several minutes later, carrying two fishing poles and a tackle-box. She stared at the rods in disbelief. 'What's all that for?' she questioned, the second he climbed into the cab.

'Fishing.'

'I know that!' Loath as she was to mention the fact, she forced herself to remind him, 'I meant... I thought we were going to have a discussion.' She gave him a hopeful smile. 'But if you'd rather fish...'

'Believe me,' he said, shooting her a sharp look, 'we'll have that talk. Consider the drive to our... discussion site as a short reprieve.'

She struggled to hide her disappointment. 'And the poles?'

'My reward for not killing you.' He gunned the engine. 'If you were smart, you'd stay real quiet and hope it takes a long time to get there.'

'But——'

'Not another word!' His words exploded with a fury that left her in no doubt as to how tenuous a hold he had on his temper. 'Woman, you are inches away from disaster. I guarantee, you don't want to push me any further.'

Taking his suggestion to heart, she didn't open her mouth the entire length of the ride. She soon realized what destination he had in mind. The rough dirt track that he turned on to led to a small, secluded lake in the far western section of the ranch. It had been one of their favorite meeting-spots eight years ago. It was also about as far from curious eyes and ears as they could get. As much as she dreaded the coming confrontation, she appreciated his determination to keep it as private as possible.

'Hunter,' she began as they neared the lake.

'Not yet,' he bit out. 'I'm still not calm enough to deal with you.'

Pulling the truck to a stop at the end of the track, he climbed from the cab and gathered up the poles, tacklebox and a plastic bucket. 'Let's go,' he called over his shoulder.

Reluctantly Leah left the truck, and rummaged in the back for something to sit on. If they were going to stay a while—and she suspected that they were—she intended to be comfortable. Spreading the colorful Mexican blanket in the grass at the edge of the shore, she removed her boots and socks and rolled her jeans to her knees. Sticking her feet into the cool water, she asked, 'Are we going to talk first or fish?'

He spared her a brief glance. 'Both. You want a rod?'

'Might as well,' she muttered.

She searched the surrounding bermuda grass until she found a good-sized cricket. Carrying it back to the blanket, she knelt beside her pole, closed her eyes, and stuck the insect on the end of the hook. Ready to catch a catfish or two, she cast toward the middle of the lake. A bright yellow and red bobber marked her spot and she settled back on the blanket, wishing she could truly relax and enjoy a lazy afternoon of fishing. But she was all too aware of their coming 'discussion'.

Hunter attached his spinner bait to his line and cast into a marshy, partially shaded section of water known to attract bass. 'I've told you before, you can't bait a hook without looking,' he informed her in a taut voice.

'I just did.'

He yanked on his line. 'One of these times, you're going to set the hook in your finger instead of the cricket. It's going to hurt. It's going to bleed. And I'm going to have to cut the damned thing out.'

'*If* that fine day ever arrives, you can say "I told you so". Until then, I'd rather not see what I'm murdering.' She cupped her chin in her hand and rested her elbow on a bent knee. 'Are we going to fight over fishing, or are we going to fight over the real problem?'

He turned his head and studied her. More than a hint of anger lingered in the depths of his eyes. 'Do you even know what that is?'

'Sure,' she said with a shrug. 'You hit Orrie.'

'You're damned right, I hit him. All things considered, he got off easy.' Hunter slowly reeled in his line. 'But that's not the issue.'

She knew it wasn't, though he'd never get her to admit it. 'Mateo loves working with the horses,' she said instead. 'Did you have to make him give it up? And why fire Lenny? He's a good worker and a wonderful man.'

Hunter cast his line again, his mouth tightening. 'Nor is that the issue.'

'It is so,' she disagreed, her frustration flaring out of control. 'It's why we're arguing.'

'No, it's not. It's why you're annoyed, but it's not why we're arguing,' he corrected harshly. 'You're annoyed because I didn't consult with you before making changes and we're arguing because I won't explain my decision.'

He'd hit the nail on the head, and she focused her attention on that particular aspect of the discussion. 'Why did you do it? Why did you fire Orrie and Lenny and change Mateo's job?' He remained stubbornly silent and she wanted to scream in exasperation. 'You're not going to tell me, are you?'

'No, I'm not.'

'Because it's not the *issue*?' she demanded, tossing her pole to the grass and scrambling to her feet. 'It's my ranch, too. I have a right to know. You promised to give everyone a fair chance. You promised!'

Setting his rod on the blanket, he reached out and swept her feet from under her, catching her before she hit the ground. '*That's* the issue,' he practically snarled. 'I made a promise to you—which I kept. And you made a promise to me—which you didn't keep.'

She fought his hold, with no success. His strength was too great. 'I don't know what you're talking about,' she insisted.

He pushed her back on to the blanket and knelt above her, planting his hands on either side of her head. 'Who's in charge of this ranch?'

'That's not the point.'

'It's precisely the point. Answer me. Who's in charge of this ranch?'

It galled her to say it. 'You are,' she forced herself to admit. She pushed against his chest, struggling to sit up. To her relief, he rocked back on to his heels, allowing her to wriggle out from beneath him.

'So you do remember our conversation at the line-shack,' he said in satisfaction.

She wrapped her arms around her waist. 'Very funny. How could I forget?' It wasn't one of her more pleasant recollections. Every last, painful detail had been burned into her memory.

'And do you also remember the promises we exchanged?'

'Of course.'

'So do I.' He ticked them off on his fingers. 'I promised to give your employees a fair chance. I promised to give your grandmother a home. And I promised to sign a prenuptial agreement. Is that everything?'

She glanced at him uneasily. 'Yes.'

'You promised one thing. What was it?'

She knew where he was headed with this and she didn't like it. 'I seem to remember there being more than one,' she temporized.

'Fine,' he said evenly. 'Name any that you remember.'

Time to face the music. She should be grateful that he wasn't rending her limb from limb. She looked him straight in the eye and said, 'I promised you'd be in charge of the ranch.'

'Which means?'

She sighed. 'That what you say goes. That I'm not to question you in front of the employees or second-guess your decisions. You don't work by committee,' she repeated his demands by rote.

'And did you do that? Did you keep your promise?'

Reluctantly she shook her head. 'No.' Nor had she kept her agreement to make their marriage a fully functioning one. She should be grateful that he hadn't pointed that out as well.

'*That's* why I'm angry. One of these days you'll trust me to do what's right for you and for the ranch. You'll trust me without question.'

'You mean blindly.'

'Okay. That's what I mean.'

She bit down on her lip. How could she do what he asked when it might all be part of an elaborate game of revenge, an attempt to even the score for old wrongs? 'I don't think I can do that, Hunter. You're asking me to risk everything.'

'Yes. I am.'

'It's too much,' she whispered, staring down at the blanket, running the wool fringe through her fingers. 'I can't give it to you. Not yet.'

A long minute ticked by before he inclined his head. 'All right. I'll answer your questions—this time.'

She glanced up in surprise. 'You'll tell me why you fired Orrie and Lenny? Why you made Mateo give up the horses?'

'Yes. This once I'll explain myself. Next time you either trust me or you don't; I don't care which. But don't expect me to defend my actions again. You understand?' At her nod, he said, 'I put Mateo in charge of the haying operation. It meant an increase in wages—something he and his family need. Plus he knows more about mechanics than he does about horses.'

'But... he knows everything about horses.'

'He knows more about repairing our equipment. As for Lenny... He wasn't happy working on a ranch. But employment meant more to him than his dislike of ranching, which says a lot about the man's character, so I recommended him for a job as a security-guard at your godfather's bank. Lenny jumped at the opportunity.'

She could hardly take it in. 'And Orrie?'

He frowned. 'Orrie was a thief,' he told her reluctantly.

'A thief! I don't believe it. What did he steal?' An obstinate look appeared in his eyes, a look she didn't doubt he'd find reflected in her own. 'Hunter?' she prompted, refusing to let it drop.

'He took your silver circlet.'

She stared in shock. 'From my wedding-gown? But that was in our...'

'Bedroom,' he finished for her.

The full implication gradually sank in. Without a word she turned away and reached for her pole. It felt as if she'd been stabbed in the back by a family member. Her betrayal went so deep that she couldn't even find the words to express it. Slowly, she brought in the line, blinking hard. The cricket was long-gone and she didn't have the stomach to kill another. At some point during their conversation she'd lost her enthusiasm for fishing.

As though sensing her distress, Hunter caught her braid and used it to reel her in. She didn't resist. Right now she needed all the comfort she could get. He folded his arms around her and she snuggled into his embrace. 'You okay?' he asked.

'No,' she replied, her voice muffled against his shirt. 'See what happens when you trust people?'

'Yes, I see. But I'm not Orrie.'

She sighed. 'No, you're not. I'm sorry, Hunter. I should have trusted you to do the right thing for the ranch.'

'Yes, you should have.'

'And I shouldn't have questioned your judgement in front of the men.'

'No, you shouldn't have. Apology accepted.' Without warning he released her, and stripped off his shirt and boots. Then, snatching her high in his arms, he walked into the lake, holding her above the water.

She clung to him, laughing. 'Don't! Don't drop me.'

'Do you trust me?'

'Blindly?'

'Is there any other way?'

She bit her lower lip. 'Okay. I trust you. Blindly.'

'Close your eyes.'

'They're closed.'

'And take a deep breath.'

'Hunter, no!' she yelped. He tossed her into the air and she tumbled, shrieking, landing in the water with a huge splash. An instant later Hunter dived in beside her, kicking with her to the surface. She gasped for air. 'I thought you said I could trust you.'

A slow grin drifted across his lean face and he caught her close. 'I never said what you could trust me to do.'

And therein lay the real crux of the matter. She knew he'd do what he thought best—but would it be right for her? As much as she wanted to believe, she couldn't. Not yet.

As they drifted toward shore her hair floated free of its braid, wrapping them in a net of long silvery tendrils. He beached them in the grass and gazed down at her, his attention snared by the wet shirt clinging to her breasts. His palm settled on the taut, supple lines of her midriff, where her shirt had parted company with her jeans. As though unable to resist he lowered his head, and gently bit the rigid peak of her breast through the wet cotton.

Her breath stopped in her throat and her nails bit into his shoulders, marking him with tiny crescent scars of passion. 'Hunter!' His name escaped her as though ripped from her throat, filled with an undeniable urgency.

He responded instantly, releasing her breast and plundering her mouth, parting her lips in search of the sweet warmth within. She couldn't seem to get enough of him. Her hands swept down his back, stroking him, needing to absorb him into her very pores, the seductive brush of cloth against skin an almost painful stimulation. His taste filled her mouth, his unique musky scent her lungs. She felt him tug at the fastening of his jeans... And then he hesitated.

Slowly he lifted his head, his angled features stark with want, dark with intent. She knew that expression, knew how close to the edge he must be. She stared at him uncertainly, caught between completing the intimacy he so clearly craved and she so desperately needed, and retreating from an act that would enable him to wrest the final bit of control from her possession. And she waited, waited for him to give in to his desire, to strip away the wet clothes and make her his wife in fact as well as name But instead he drew away, and she could only imagine the amount of willpower it must have taken him

He kissed her again, the caress hard and swift. 'Not here. Not like this. But soon,' he warned in a determined voice. 'Very soon. When there are no more doubts in your mind...when there's no chance of turning back, we will finish this and you will be mine.'

She didn't argue. How could she? He was right. Soon they would be lovers, and if she wasn't very, very careful she'd lose her heart as surely as she was losing control of the ranch. And, when that happened, Hunter would finally have his revenge.

The next few days passed with a comfortable ease that gave Leah hope for the future. Hunter continued to work with Dreamseeker, though whether or not he'd made any headway with the stallion was a topic of hot debate. Still, she didn't doubt who would eventually win their battle of wills.

To her relief, the employees seemed quite content working under Hunter's management. Losing two wranglers left ample work for everyone, and she suspected that the fear of being laid off had finally dissipated. Mateo was far happier than she'd ever seen him. And dropping in on Lenny in his new position as security-guard proved that Hunter had been right about that change as well.

Returning from the bank late one cloudy afternoon, she was surprised to discover Hunter Rototilling the ground around the porch. The powerful blades bit into the dark soil, grinding up the crushed remains of Grandmother Rose's begonias.

'What are you doing?' she called. He didn't answer, merely lifted a hand in greeting and resumed his work. Inez stood on the porch and Leah joined her. 'What's he doing?' she asked the housekeeper. 'Or perhaps I should ask why. Why is he plowing the garden under?'

'*No sé*,' Inez replied with a shrug. 'Abuela Rosa, she took one look, said a nasty word, and stomped off to the kitchen. I don't think she is happy that Señor Pryde has decided to ruin her garden.'

Leah frowned. 'Hunter isn't ruining her garden; Bull Jones took care of that already. Hunter's just finishing the job.'

Rose appeared in the doorway, carrying a tray with a pitcher of iced tea and glasses. 'If we're going to stand around and watch all my hard work being ground into mulch, we might as well be comfortable.'

Leah hastened to take the tray, setting it on a low wrought-iron table. 'There wasn't much left to mulch,' she reassured, pouring drinks and handing them around. 'Our neighboring foreman made sure of that.'

With a noisy humph, Rose sat in a rocker. 'If Hunter thinks I'm starting over again, he's got another think coming. That garden can grow rocks and weeds for all I care.' She took a sip of tea. 'What's he doing over there? What's in those bags?'

'*Es abono, sí*?' Inez suggested.

'Fertilizer, huh?' Rose slowly rocked in her chair. 'Yes, sir. That'll give him a fine crop of weeds. A truly fine crop.' She craned her neck. 'Where's he going now?'

Leah shrugged, frowning as Hunter walked toward the rear of the house. 'I don't know. Maybe he's through for the day.'

'Through!' Rose rocked a little faster. 'With everything such a mess? He'd better not leave my garden like that, or I'll have a thing or two to say about it. See if I don't.'

Leah jumped to her feet and leaned over the rail. 'False alarm. Here he comes. He was just pulling the pick-up around.' He climbed out of the cab and crossed to the back of the truck. Lowering the tailgate, he removed an assortment of bedding plants. She glanced over her shoulder at Rose. 'He bought jasmine for the trellis. I adore jasmine.'

Inez joined her at the railing, beaming in delight. '*Y mira*!'

Slowly Rose stood. 'Well, I'll be. He bought some roses.'

Leah began to laugh. 'How appropriate. They're peace roses.'

Hunter lined the plants around the perimeter of the house, then approached, carrying a shovel. He stood at the bottom of the porch steps and looked directly at Rose. 'Well? You going to play lady of the manor, or do you want to get your hands dirty and help?'

Rose lifted her chin. 'Whose garden is it?' she demanded.

Hunter shrugged. 'I'm no gardener. Just thought I'd get it started.'

'In that case, I'll fetch my gloves,' she agreed. At the door she paused, and with a crotchety glare demanded, 'Don't you break ground without me. Hear?'

Leah waited until Rose was out of earshot before approaching Hunter, offering him a glass of iced tea. 'This is very thoughtful of you. When Bull destroyed her last flowerbed, she gave in to the inevitable and didn't try again.'

He drank the tea and handed her the empty glass. 'He won't destroy another.'

She didn't doubt it for a minute. 'Peace roses?' she asked, raising an eyebrow.

He tipped his hat to the back of his head with a gloved finger, and in that moment, Leah didn't think she'd ever seen him look more attractive. 'Yeah, well. I figured it was past time we came to terms. We'll stick in a few rose bushes and talk. Before we're done we'll have worked out our differences.'

Leah smiled. 'I'm sure you will,' she said softly. 'It's just difficult for her to adjust to all the changes.'

'I'm not done making them, you know,' he warned.

She nodded. 'I know.'

He'd never promised not to make changes. But they were for the better. And more and more she realized how important he'd become—to her employees, to the ranch...even to her grandmother, loath as Rose might be to admit it.

But most of all, he'd become important to her, perhaps even vital. And before much longer she'd have to deal with that knowledge.

Leah watched in concern the next morning as Hunter and his men drove one of the ranch bulls into a pen in preparation for transporting him to his new owner. She'd nicknamed the animal 'Red' because of his tendency to charge anything or anyone foolish enough to wear that color. After nearly being gored by the bull, Hunter had decided to sell the animal.

He'd also flatly refused to allow her to help move Red to the pen, saying it was 'much too dangerous'. She'd heard that phrase used more than once and had rapidly grown to hate it. But she didn't dare argue, especially in front of the employees and especially when—in this particular case—he was right. The bull was very dangerous.

She climbed to the top rail of the corral fence and looked on from a safe distance. With Red secure and peaceful in the holding-pen, the men only awaited the arrival of the truck to move the bull to his new home.

'Señora Leah!' came a childish shout from behind her. 'Silkie! Get Silkie.'

She turned in time to see all six Arroya children chasing after their new sheepdog puppy. The tiny animal, yapping for all she was worth, streaked beneath the rail of the corral, barreling straight toward the holding-pen...and the bull. And around her neck, bouncing in the dust, hung a huge, red floppy bow.

'Stay there!' she called over her shoulder, hopping off the rail. 'Don't you dare come into the corral. You understand?'

The children obediently skidded to a halt and nodded as one. Six pairs of huge dark eyes stared at her, wide with mingled fear and hope. Wincing at their trusting expressions, Leah hotfooted it after the wayward puppy.

Across the corral the dog ran, and Leah realized that she'd have only one chance to catch the animal before it was too late. At the last possible second, just as they reached the holding-pen, she flung herself at Silkie. Belly-flopping to a dusty halt, inches from the bottom rail, her hand closed around the furry, struggling puppy. For a brief second she held the animal safely in her grasp. Then, with a frantic wiggle, Silkie scrambled free and scooted beneath the rail.

'Silkie, no!' she yelled.

Set on a course of total annihilation, the puppy darted toward the bull. Taking a deep breath and whispering a fervent prayer, Leah ducked beneath the rail, hoping she could snag the animal and escape unscathed. A hard, relentless hand landed on her arm and jerked her back, spinning her around. She stared up into Hunter's furious face.

'Are you nuts?' he practically roared.

'The puppy!' she cried, fighting his hold. 'I've got to save the puppy!'

He glanced from Leah to the Arroya children. 'Open the gates!' he shouted to his men. 'Get the bull out of there!'

Yelling and whistling, the wranglers unlatched the gate between the holding-pen and the pasture. But the bull didn't notice. Focused entirely on Silkie, he lowered his head, pawing at the ground and bellowing in fury. He scored the ground with his horns, just missing the dog.

Swearing beneath his breath, Hunter tossed his hat to the ground and ripped off his shirt. Before anyone could stop him, he climbed beneath the rail and entered the holding-pen.

'Hunter, don't do it!' Leah started to follow, but the look on his face stopped her. If she moved another step, she'd divert his attention and the bull would kill him. It was that simple. She clasped her trembling hands together, hardly daring to breathe. With a fervor bordering on hysteria, she began to pray.

Waving his shirt in the air, Hunter caught the bull's attention. Distracted by this new, more accessible target, the huge animal instantly charged. At the last possible second Hunter threw his shirt at the bull's head and, diving to one side, rolled clear of the vicious hooves and horns. Red pounded by and Hunter leapt to his feet. Snagging the puppy by the scruff of her neck, he vaulted over the fence to safety.

Blinded, Red crashed into the fence between the holding-pen and the corral, the rails splintering beneath the impact. Keeping Silkie tucked safely under his arm, Hunter grabbed Leah by the wrist and ran flat out for the far side of the corral. The bull stood close to the splintered rails, blowing hard. With several shakes of his head he reduced the shirt covering him to rags. Then he looked around for his next victim. At long last, he spied

did trust him, she realized. She trusted him every bit as much as she loved him. Blindly. Totally. Completely.

And she'd never been more frightened in her life. For Hunter had it all now...the ranch and her heart. The only question was...what would he do when he found out?

CHAPTER EIGHT

EARLY the next morning Lyon Enterprises' latest offer arrived by special messenger. Gazing in fury at the papers, Leah knocked back the kitchen chair and went in search of Hunter. Eventually she tracked him down in the barn, running a curry-comb over his buckskin.

'Look at this,' she said, holding out the white embossed envelope.

He set aside his equipment and took the papers, scanning them. His mouth tightened briefly, then he shrugged. 'So? Either write your acceptance or trash it.'

She stared in disbelief as he guided his gelding from the grooming-box and returned the horse to his stall. 'That's it? That's all you're going to say?' she demanded, trailing behind.

He shouldered past her and crossed the barn aisle to a stack of hay bales. Using two large hooks, he lifted a bale and carried it to the stall. 'What do you want me to say?'

She regarded him with frustration. 'Something more than what you have. I'm tired of their pestering me. I'd think you would be, too. Or don't you care if I sell out to them?'

He released a gusty sigh and glanced over his shoulder at her. 'Is that what you want? To sell? I thought the whole point of marrying was to prevent Lyon from getting their hands on your ranch.'

'It was, but you seem so...' She shrugged. 'I don't know. Detached.'

'I am. It's not my ranch.'

133

She wasn't sure why she kept pushing it. But something about his careless indifference didn't quite ring true. After all, he'd also married in order to secure the ranch. She didn't believe for one minute that he was as unconcerned about her accepting Lyon's offer as he claimed. 'So you wouldn't object if I sold to them.'

'No.' He paused in his labors. 'Though legally you can't without offering me first refusal.'

She blinked, momentarily sidetracked. 'Come again?'

He rolled up his sleeves and leaned his arms on the stall door, exposing the powerful muscles of his forearms. 'The prenup, remember? You retain title of the ranch in the event of a divorce. But if you choose to sell, I have right of first refusal.' He frowned at her, tilting his hat to the back of his head. 'You're the one who insisted we sign the damned thing. Didn't you even bother to read it?'

'Yes.' No. She'd just signed where her lawyer had told her in order to get it over and done with.

'Yeah, right,' he said, clearly not believing her. 'You should have read it, Leah. There are one or two other important clauses in there that you should be familiar with. If that's the way you conduct all your business, it's a wonder you weren't bankrupt years ago.'

She hadn't come to argue. She'd come to vent her anger over Lyon Enterprises' non-stop harassment—an anger that had finally reached the boiling point. 'That's not what's at issue,' she said, determined to get the conversation back on track. 'I'd like to discuss this offer.'

'So discuss it. I'm listening.'

She took a deep breath. 'I plan to drive to Houston this week and talk to them.'

That stopped him. 'You *what*?'

'I want to have it out once and for all—tell them I won't sell.'

He stared at her as though she'd lost her mind. 'If you don't want to sell, just trash the thing. You don't need to drive all the way to Houston to do that. Last time I looked you kept a wastebasket in the study. Use that one.'

'Very funny. I have to go to Houston.'

'Why?'

'So I can address the Lyon Enterprises board.'

He froze for a split-second, the check in his movements so brief she almost missed it. Leaving the stall, he slung the remains of the bale on to the stack and crossed to her side. His hat brim threw his face into shadow, but she could see the dark glitter of his eyes and the taut line of his jaw. Was he angry? She couldn't quite tell.

'And why,' he asked softly, 'would you want to address the board of Lyon Enterprises?'

Her voice sharpened. 'I've had it with these people. As far as I'm concerned this latest offer is the final straw. I'm not putting up with it any more. I'm going to make it clear that I won't be entertaining any future offers and that I won't sell to them. Ever. If necessary I'll even tell them what you said—that our prenuptial agreement gives you first right of refusal.'

He shook his head. 'Over my dead body. That's nobody's business but ours.'

'Okay,' she conceded, uncertain of his temperament. Any time his voice dropped to such a low, husky note she tended to tread warily. 'But I still want to go to Houston and talk to them. And I want you to go with me.'

'Why?' he said again.

She glanced at him uncertainly. 'To support me, if you're willing.'

He turned away, resting a booted foot on the haystack. She could tell from the tense set of his shoulders that she'd thrown him, and she studied his expressionless profile in concern. Perhaps she'd pushed it by requesting his support. If only she could read his thoughts, she'd know. But he'd always been exceptionally successful at keeping them hidden from her.

Finally he nodded. 'Okay. I'll go. We'll leave Friday and spend the weekend at my apartment.'

'You have an apartment in Houston?' she asked in astonishment.

'You can see for yourself when we get there.' His brows drew together. 'Leah, I need you to agree to something.'

She eyed him warily. 'What?'

He stripped off his gloves and tucked them into his belt. 'Once you've confronted the board, I want to handle the situation from then on.'

'But it's not your problem.'

'Yes, it is. Anything that affects this ranch is my problem. And dealing with companies like Lyon Enterprises is my area of expertise—my former area of expertise.'

'Do you think you can get them to leave me alone?'

'No. But I can do a good job of holding them at bay. I'm better equipped than you to wage this war.'

Suddenly she recalled her need for a knight on a white charger, battling the nasty dragon in order to save the damsel in distress. When Hunter had shown up she'd been sure he was the dragon, and that she'd have to fight her own battles. Now she wondered. Perhaps they'd fight those battles together, and Lyon Enterprises would be vanquished once and for all.

'Let me have my say, and then it's your problem,' she promised.

'Fine.' He dropped an arm across her shoulders. 'I'm starved. How about you?'

She grinned. It felt as though the weight of the world had been lifted from her shoulders. 'I think I could eat a horse,' she confessed, and walked with him to the house.

Late that night Hunter lifted the phone receiver and punched in a series of numbers. A minute later Kevin answered.

'It's me,' Hunter said. 'I'm coming in. Call the board together.'

'What's wrong?' Kevin demanded. 'What happened?'

'Leah received Lyon's latest offer and wants to meet with them.'

'She *what*?'

'You heard me.'

'What the hell are you going to do?'

'Introduce her to the board of Lyon Enterprises, what else?'

'I mean . . . what are *you* going to do? What if . . . what if she finds out?'

'She won't.' Hunter spoke with absolute confidence.

'Why not?'

'Because no one would dare tell her anything.'

'If they think it'll help with the sale——'

'Once they meet her, they'll see that she trusts me,' Hunter cut in briskly. 'And they'll realize it's to their advantage to keep quiet. Telling her who I am won't help their cause any, and they're smart enough to know it.'

A long moment of silence followed while Kevin mulled over Hunter's words. 'You could be right. You usually are. I'll tell everyone you're coming.'

'And open up the apartment. We'll be spending the weekend there.'

'Won't she be suspicious? It's not precisely a poor man's pad.'

'She'll have other things on her mind by that time.'

Kevin gave a knowing chuckle. 'Understood. See you Friday.'

'Right.'

Hunter hung up and leaned back in the chair. Matters were rapidly coming to a head. More than anything he'd like to get this situation over and done with, but some things just couldn't be rushed. And this, though he'd prefer it otherwise, was one of them.

He heard a soft knock and Leah opened the door. 'Busy?' she asked.

'No. Come on in.'

She stepped into the room, standing just outside the spill of lamplight and wearing a knee-length cotton nightshirt. Unfortunately, this one wasn't the least transparent. His mouth tightened. As much as he enjoyed seeing his wife in next to nothing, he couldn't have her running around half-dressed. One of these days he'd need to make a serious effort to break her of the habit.

'Who were you talking to?' she asked.

'A business associate.'

She came closer. Her hair, cascading past her waist, caught the light from the desk lamp and gleamed like fallen moonbeams. 'Is there a problem?'

He shook his head. 'Just thought I'd tell him I'd be in town at the end of the week.'

'Oh.' She stood a little uncertainly in the middle of the room. 'Are you coming to bed soon?'

He shoved back the chair and walked toward her. 'Is now soon enough?'

'Yes.' She couldn't quite meet his eyes and he felt her sudden tension.

He reached her side and stared down into her face. He'd never seen such perfection. Her eyes glowed like amethysts, her heart-shaped face full of strength and character and determination. 'I want to make love to you,' he told her bluntly, thrusting his fingers into the silken fall of her hair. 'I've been patient long enough.'

She twisted her hands together. 'I know. But...'

'Friday,' he stated, catching her chin with his knuckle and forcing her to look at him. 'I want a decision by Friday, Leah. You have to commit at some point.'

Slowly she nodded. 'Okay. Friday. We'll meet with the Lyon board and then have the rest of the weekend to ourselves.'

He smiled in satisfaction. 'Done. And now, wife, it's time for bed.' He slid an arm around her and lifted her close. She trembled in his arms, which told him more than anything his effect on her.

'Hunter——'

He sensed that her nervousness had gotten the better of her, that given the opportunity she'd rescind her agreement. He stopped her words with a swift, rough kiss, then took her mouth again in a second, slower, more thorough kiss—a precursory taste of the pleasure he intended to share with her over the weekend.

They left early on Friday, arranging to meet with the Lyon personnel after lunch. Leah had dressed carefully, choosing a pearl-gray suit, matching pumps and a white silk blouse. To add a touch of sophistication, she'd looped her hair into a businesslike chignon, and as a morale booster displayed the necklace Hunter had given her as a wedding-gift.

To her surprise, Hunter dressed casually, exchanging his jeans for cotton trousers, his plaid shirt no different from the ones he wore when working. The boa tie he'd strung around his neck was his only concession to the occasion.

'Relax,' he said, driving toward the Post Oak section of Houston. 'They won't eat you.'

Her expression felt stiff and unnatural. 'I'm more concerned about them slitting my throat,' she attempted to joke. 'Especially after I tell them not to contact me ever again.'

'Too obvious. They'll just sell you off to white slavers.' He looked at her and sighed. 'I'm kidding, honey.'

'Oh.' She grinned weakly and her hand closed over the pendant; she was hoping it would give her even a minuscule amount of Hunter's strength and perseverance. 'I'm beginning to think this isn't such a great idea.'

He spared her another brief glance. 'You want to turn back?'

'No. Maybe if I do this they'll finally leave me alone.' She shifted in her seat and studied Hunter's profile. 'Do you think they will? Leave me alone, I mean?'

He shrugged. 'They might. But don't count on it. They're businessmen. All they care about is the bottom line on the balance sheet. If buying your ranch means a substantial profit, then no. They won't leave you alone.'

A small frown knit her brow. 'I'll have to think of a way to convince them I mean business.'

'Short of a stick of dynamite between their ears, I don't know how.'

His comment gave her an idea and a secretive smile crept across her mouth. 'I'm not so sure about the dynamite, although the idea has merit. Perhaps a slightly less drastic demonstration would be in order.' Opening the glove compartment, she rummaged around until she found what she sought. Without a word, she pocketed the item, hoping Hunter hadn't noticed the furtive act.

A few minutes later he pointed out a tall, modern glass building with smoked windows. 'That's where we're headed,' he told her, pulling into an underground parking-lot.

Leaving the car, they took the garage elevator to the lobby. 'Which floor is Lyon Enterprises?' Leah asked.

'All of them.'

She stopped dead in her tracks. 'They own the *building*?'

'They're a large company. Lots of companies own entire buildings.' He cupped her elbow and ushered her along. 'Come on. We want the executive level.'

She clutched her purse and the large white envelope with Lyon's offer to her chest. She hadn't realized. She'd had no idea they were such an immense concern. Suddenly she felt very small and vulnerable. How could she ever hope to defeat this Goliath of a company? She was no David. She glanced at Hunter. But he was. He'd protect her. All she had to do was trust him.

Filled with renewed confidence, she walked with him to the security desk. After presenting their credentials, they were escorted to a private bank of elevators that carried them directly to the executive level. Inside the car, she tucked back an escaped wisp of hair and straightened her skirt.

Hunter caught her hand, stilling her nervous exertions. 'Listen to me, Leah. These corporate types eat people like you for a midnight snack. So, don't fidget. Keep your arms relaxed at your side unless you're handing them something. Look them straight in the eye. Think before you speak. Don't answer any question you don't want to. And above all don't lose your temper. Got it?'

Her tension eased. 'Got it.'

His mouth curled to one side and she realized in amazement that he actually relished the coming confrontation. 'Remember, I'll support you every step of the way. The instant you get in too deep, I'll bail you out. Otherwise, it's your show.'

'Hunter?'

He lifted an eyebrow. 'What?'

She squeezed his hand. 'Thanks.'

'Don't thank me, Leah,' he said, and the seriousness of his tone gave his words an ominous weight. 'Not yet.'

The doors slid open and she released her death grip on him. It wouldn't do for the Lyon board to think that she needed his assistance, even if she did. Stepping from the car, they found a secretary awaiting their arrival.

'Welcome to Lyon Enterprises,' she said. 'You're expected, of course. If you'd follow me?'

She led the way to a pair of wide, double doors. Pushing them open, she gestured for Hunter and Leah to enter. As though in a calculated gesture, the doors banged closed behind, barring their exit. A huge glass table dominated the conference room, and around the table sat a dozen men and women. The man at the far end rose to his feet.

'Miss Hampton,' he said. 'A pleasure to finally meet you. I'm Buddy Peterson. Our chairman requested that I conduct these proceedings, if you have no objections.'

She did object. She wanted to speak directly to the head honcho. 'He's not here?'

'He preferred that I negotiate in his place.' It didn't quite answer her question, but from long experience with Hunter she knew she wouldn't get a more direct response. 'Pryde,' Peterson said, switching his attention to Hunter. 'We were somewhat surprised to hear you'd be attending this meeting—with Miss Hampton, that is.'

'Were you?' Hunter replied. 'I don't know why, considering Leah's my wife.'

'Your *wife*!' The board members exchanged quick glances and Peterson slowly sank back into his seat. 'This puts a slightly different complexion on matters.'

Hunter inclined his head. 'Yes, it does, doesn't it?'

Peterson laughed, a cynical expression gleaming in his eyes. 'Congratulations... I'm impressed. I couldn't have done better myself.'

Leah looked up at Hunter in confusion. 'They know you?' she murmured.

'We're acquainted.'

'You didn't tell me.'

'It wasn't important.' His dark, unfathomable gaze captured hers. 'Do you have something to say to these people?'

She nodded. 'Yes.'

'Then get to it.'

She felt like a pawn in a game without rules. She glanced at Hunter, sudden doubts assailing her, acutely aware that she'd missed a vital piece of information, a clue that would help explain the mysterious undercurrents shifting through the room. She also suspected that what had to be said already had been, though in a language she couldn't hope to decipher. What she chose to contribute would be considered, at best, an empty gesture. Still, she wouldn't have this opportunity ever again. She wanted to say something they'd remember... do something they'd remember. She wanted them to know that Leah Hampton Pryde had been here and made a statement.

Taking a deep breath, she stepped to the table and held out the envelope. 'This arrived the other day.'

'Yes, our offer,' Peterson said with an impatient edge. 'Don't tell me you plan to accept?' He glanced at Hunter. 'It would certainly save much of this board's time and energy if you would.'

'Not only do I not accept, I don't want to hear from you ever again. You people have harassed me for the last time. I'm not the vulnerable woman struggling on my own any more.' She spared Hunter a quick, searching look. At his brief nod, she added, 'I have help now. We won't allow Bull Jones to foul our wells or stampede our herd. We won't be intimidated by you any longer.'

'Yes, yes,' Buddy Peterson interrupted, 'you've made your point.'

'Not yet, I haven't.'

She reached into her suit jacket pocket and pulled out the lighter she'd taken from the glove compartment. With a flick of her thumb she spun the wheel, and a small flame leapt to life. Stepping closer, she held the flame beneath the corner of the envelope and waited until it caught fire. Then she tossed the burning packet into the center of the glass table. Flames and smoke billowed. Frantic executives scrambled from their seats, shouting and cursing.

Beside her, Hunter sighed. 'You really shouldn't have done that.'

She lifted her chin. 'Yes, I should have. *Now* I've made my point.'

'That ... and more.'

'Good. Are you ready to leave?'

To her bewilderment, he shot a chary glance at the ceiling, pulled his hat lower over his brow and raised the collar of his shirt. 'In a minute. Go to the car. I'll be right behind.'

The instant the door closed behind her an alarm bell began to scream and the overhead sprinklers burst to life. In a mad dash the executives scurried from the room, like rats deserting a sinking ship.

'Get these sprinklers turned off!' Buddy Peterson bellowed. He continued to sit at the table, his arms folded across his chest, ignoring the drenching spray. 'That was damned clever, Hunter,' he called above the screeching siren.

'She does have a certain...flair, doesn't she?' Hunter said, impervious to the water funneling in a small waterfall from his hat brim.

Peterson stood and approached. 'That's not what I meant, and you know it. How long are you going to keep her in the dark—not tell her who you really are?'

'As long as it takes.'

'You're playing a dangerous game. You could lose everything,' Peterson advised.

'I don't lose.' Hunter's voice dropped, a hard, threatening note coloring his words. 'Fair warning. One leak from anyone at this table and you'll all suffer the consequences. I'll be in touch soon.' He didn't wait for a response. Turning, he left.

'I still don't understand how you got so wet.'

'I told you. A freak shower.'

'Where? There isn't a cloud in the sky.' Sarcasm crept into her voice. 'Or perhaps it rained somewhere between the executive floor and the garage.'

He released a soft laugh. 'Something like that.'

She gave up. Hunter could be incredibly close-mouthed when he chose. If he'd decided that he wouldn't tell her, then he wouldn't. It was that simple. 'What did you say to the board after I left?'

He swung into another parking garage, this one beneath a brand-new, high-rise apartment complex. 'Not much. They didn't hang around for long.'

'Hunter!' she exclaimed in exasperation. 'Why won't you give me a straight answer? What did you say? How do you know them? For that matter, how did you know your way around their building? And why all the secrecy?'

He pulled into a wide parking space with H. Pryde stencilled on to the wall above it. Switching off the engine, he rested his arms on the steering-wheel and turned and looked at her. 'I know the Lyon board through work, which is also how I knew my way around their complex. I told Peterson that I'd be in touch soon. And I'm not being in the least secretive—just selective in what I tell you.'

'Why?'

'Because Lyon is my problem now, and I'll handle it.'

She could accept that. Having to deal all these years with the constant stream of difficulties on the ranch, it was a welcome change to have a second set of shoulders to help carry the burden. 'Why did you tell Buddy Peterson you'd be in touch?'

'To make certain he doesn't bother you again.'

'And he'll agree to that?' she asked in amazement.

'I won't give him any choice.' He opened his door. 'Coming?'

After unloading their overnight bags, Hunter led the way to the bank of elevators. Once there, he keyed the security lock for the penthouse and Leah stiffened. 'The penthouse?'

He paused before answering, and for some reason his momentary hesitation made her think of his advice about addressing the board members of Lyon Enterprises. 'Think before you speak,' he'd told her. 'Don't answer any question you don't want to.' Perhaps that advice didn't apply solely to board members. Perhaps it applied to recalcitrant wives as well.

'They paid me well in my previous job,' he finally said.

'I guess so. I'm surprised you left.' The car glided rapidly upward and she peeked at him from beneath her lashes. 'But that's right... You said you'd still do occasional jobs for them if they called. Troubleshooting, isn't that your speciality?'

'Yes.'

'What did you say the name of the company was?'

'I didn't.' He leaned back against the wall and folded his arms across his chest. 'Why all the questions, Leah?'

'You can't expect me not to have questions.' Her grip on her purse tightened. 'I'm... surprised.'

'Because I'm not the dirt-poor ranch-hand I once was?'

She shot him a sharp look. 'We've been over this before. That's not the problem and you know it. You ask me to trust you. To trust you blindly. But you tell me nothing about yourself, which means *you* don't trust *me*.'

'Point taken,' he conceded.

The doors slid silently apart, opening on to a huge entrance hall. Swallowing nervously, she stepped out of the car. 'Good heavens, Hunter, look at this place!'

'I've seen it before, remember?' he said gently. 'Make yourself at home.'

Her heels clicked on the oak parquet flooring as she crossed to the sunken living-room. 'Why didn't you tell me?' she asked quietly. 'Why the games?'

His hat sailed past her, skimming the coffee-table and landing dead-center in the middle of the *chaise longue*. 'All right. I admit I may have omitted a detail or two about my life these past eight years.'

'A detail or two?' she questioned with irony.

'Or three. What difference does it make? I have money. And I have an apartment in Houston. So what?'

'It's a penthouse apartment,' she was quick to remind him.

He shrugged irritably. 'Fine. It's a penthouse apartment. It doesn't change a damned thing. We're still married. I still work the ranch. And you're still my wife.'

'Am I?'

He thrust a hand through his hair. 'What the hell is that supposed to mean?'

'Why did you marry me, Hunter?'

'You know why.'

She nodded. 'For the ranch. Perhaps also for a bit of revenge. But what I don't understand is...why? Why would you care about such a small concern when you have all this?' He didn't respond, and she realized that she could stand there until doomsday and he wouldn't answer her questions. She picked up her overnight bag. 'I'd like to freshen up. Where do I go?'

'Down the hallway. Third door on the right.'

She didn't look back. Walking away, she fought an unease—an unease she couldn't express and chose not to analyze fully. The door he'd indicated was to the master bedroom. She closed herself in the adjoining bathroom and stripped off her clothes, indulging in a quick, refreshing shower. Slipping on a bathrobe, she returned to the bedroom.

She stood beside the bed for several minutes before giving into temptation. Climbing on top of the down coverlet, she curled up in the center and shut her eyes. A short catnap would do her a world of good. But, despite the best of intentions, her thoughts kept returning to Hunter and their conversation.

The situation between them grew more and more confusing with each passing day. Standing in the middle of the penthouse living-room, seeing the visual proof of the wealth and power she'd long suspected, had forced her to face facts. Hunter Pryde had returned to the ranch for a reason . . . a reason he'd chosen not to share with her.

And no matter how hard she tried to fight it, the same question drummed incessantly in the back of her mind. Having so much, what in heaven's name did he want with her and Hampton Homestead . . . if not revenge?

CHAPTER NINE

'LEAH? Wake up, sweetheart.'

She stirred, pulled from the most delicious dream of laughter and peace roses and babies with ebony hair and eyes. She looked up to find Hunter sitting beside her on the bed. He must have showered recently; his hair was damp and slicked back from his brow, drawing attention to his angled bone-structure. He'd also discarded his shirt and wore faded jeans that rode low on his hips and emphasized his lean, muscular build. He bent closer, smoothing her hair from her eyes, and his amulet caught the light, glowing a rich blue against his deeply bronzed chest.

'What time is it?' she murmured, stretching.

'Time for dinner. You've been sleeping for two hours.'

'That long?' She sat up, adjusting the gaping robe. 'I should get dressed.'

'Don't bother on my account,' he said with a slow grin. 'I thought we'd go casual tonight.'

She wrinkled her nose. 'I suspect this might be considered a little too casual.'

'Only one person will see.' He held out his hand. 'Let me show you.'

Curious, she slipped her fingers into his and clambered off the bed. He returned to the living-room and gestured toward a spiral staircase she'd failed to notice earlier. 'Follow me.' At the top he blocked her path. 'Close your eyes and hold on,' he instructed.

'Why?'

'You'll see.'

'Okay. Don't let me fall.'

Before she knew what he intended, he scooped her up into his arms. 'Trust, remember?' he murmured against her ear. A few minutes later he set her on her feet. 'You can look now.'

She opened her eyes and gasped in disbelief. They stood on the roof of the apartment building, but it was unlike any rooftop she'd ever seen. If she hadn't known better, she'd have sworn they stood in the middle of a park. Grass grew beneath her feet and everywhere she glanced were flowers—barrels of petunias, pansies and impatiens. Even irises and tulips bloomed in profusion.

'I thought you said you weren't a gardener,' she accused.

'I lied,' he said with a careless shrug. He indicated a greenhouse occupying one end of the roof. 'Some of the more delicate flowers are grown there. But I've had an outside concern take over since I moved to the ranch. They prepared everything for our visit.'

'It's...it's incredible.'

'Hungry?'

Suddenly she realized that she was. 'Starving,' she admitted.

'I thought we'd eat here. You can change if you want, but it isn't necessary.'

She caught the underlying message. She could dine in nothing but a robe, just as he dined in nothing but jeans, or she could dress and use her clothes as a shield, a subtle way of distancing herself.

'This is fine,' she said casually. 'Satisfy my curiosity, though. What sort of meal goes with scruffiness and bare feet?'

'A picnic, of course.'

He pointed to a secluded corner where a blanket had already been spread on the grass. All around the sheltered nook were pots and pots of azaleas, heavy with blossoms in every conceivable shade. A bucket anchored one corner of the blanket, the top of a champagne bottle thrusting out of the ice. Next to the champagne she saw a huge wicker basket covered with a red-checked square of linen.

She chuckled at the cliché. 'Fried chicken?' she guessed.

'Coleslaw and potato salad,' he confirmed.

'Fast food?'

He looked insulted. 'Catered.' Crossing to their picnic spot, he knelt beside the basket and unloaded the goodies on to china.

'You're kidding,' she said in disbelief, joining him on the blanket. 'China? For a picnic?'

He gave her a bland smile. 'Isn't that what you use?'

'Not likely.' She examined the champagne. 'Perrier Jouet flower bottle? Lalique flutes? Hunter, I'm almost afraid to touch anything.' She stared at him helplessly. 'Why are you doing this?'

'It seemed ... appropriate.'

She bowed her head, her emotions threatening to shatter her self-control. 'Thank you,' she whispered. 'It's beautiful.'

'You're hungry,' he said, and she wondered if she just imagined the tenderness in his voice. 'Try this.'

He held out a succulent sliver of chicken that he'd stripped from the bone. She took it from him and almost groaned aloud. He was right. This didn't come close to fast food. She'd never tasted chicken with such a light, delicate flavor. Drawing her knees up against her chest, she tucked into the next piece he offered.

'Don't you trust me with the china?' she teased.

He extended a forkful of potato salad. 'Not when I'm seducing you.'

'With potatoes and fried chicken?' She nibbled the potato salad and this time did groan aloud. 'Ignore that question. This is delicious.'

'Want more?' At her eager nod, he patted the spot next to him. 'Then come closer.'

With a laugh she scrambled across the blanket to his side, and before long they shared a plate between them, exchanging finger food and dispensing with silverware whenever possible. Finally replete, she didn't resist when he drew her down so her head rested in his lap.

'Look at the sunset,' she said, gesturing at the vivid colors streaking across the sky above them.

'That's one of the reasons we're eating out here.' He filled a flute with champagne. Impaling a strawberry on the rim, he handed it to her. 'There's dessert.'

'No, thanks.' She sipped the champagne. 'This is all I need.' His fingers slipped into her hair and she closed her eyes beneath the delicate stroke of his hand, his abdomen warm against her cheek.

'Leah, watch,' he murmured.

She glanced up at the sky. As the last touch of purple faded into black, tiny pinpricks of light flickered to life around the rooftop. It was as though the stars had fallen from the heavens and been scattered like glittering dewdrops among the flowers. She raised a trembling hand to her mouth.

'Hunter, why?' She couldn't phrase the question any clearer, but he seemed to understand what she asked.

'I wanted tonight to be perfect.'

She released a shaky laugh. 'You succeeded.'

'Good. Because I'm going to make love to you and I want it to be special. Very special.' He made no move to carry out his promise. Instead he sat motionless, apparently enjoying the serenity of the evening. 'Eight years ago you told your grandmother about our meeting at the line-shack, didn't you?' he asked unexpectedly.

It was the last question she had ever envisioned him broaching. She didn't even consider lying to protect Rose. 'Yes.'

'You came to the line-shack and waited for me.'

'Yes,' she admitted again.

'When did you find out I'd been arrested?'

'When you told me.'

'I was afraid of that.' He released a long sigh. 'I owe you an apology, Leah. I didn't believe you. I thought you were lying about what happened back then.'

'Did Grandmother Rose tell you the truth?'

'Yes. She told me.'

'I'm glad.' Leah hesitated, then said, 'There's also an explanation for why I wouldn't leave with you—if you're willing to listen.'

The muscles in his jaw tightened, but he nodded. 'I'm listening.'

'I told my grandmother about our meeting because I couldn't leave without saying goodbye to her. That was when I learned about Dad. He was dying of cancer, Hunter. I had to stay and help take care of him. That's why I wouldn't have gone with you. But I would have asked you to come back . . . afterward.' She stared at him with nervous dread. 'I hope you believe me, because it's the truth.'

For a long time he remained silent. Then he spoke in a low, rough voice, the words sounding as though they were torn from him. 'Growing up in an orphanage, honesty came in short supply. So did trust. No one cared much about the truth, just about finding a culprit.'

'And were you usually the culprit?' she asked compassionately.

'Not always. But often enough.'

'Didn't you try and explain?'

'Why?' he asked simply. 'No one would have believed me. I was a mongrel. Not that I was innocent, you understand. I provoked my share of trouble.'

She could believe he had, though she suspected that the trouble he'd provoked had never been undeserved. 'And then one day...' she prompted.

'How did you know there was a "one day"?'

She shrugged. 'It makes sense.' She felt his laugh rumble beneath her ear.

'You're right. Okay. One day—on my fifteenth birthday, as a matter of fact—they accused me of doing something I didn't. It was the last time that happened.'

'What did they accuse you of?'

'Breaking a snow crystal—remember, those globes you shake and the little flakes swirl around inside? This one had a knight fighting a dragon.'

She stilled. 'A knight and a dragon?'

'Yes. I'd always been fascinated by the crystal, but it belonged to one of the live-in workers and was off-limits. When it broke, I took the rap.'

'But you didn't break it.'

'No.'

'Why was that the last time they accused you?'

'I left. For good.'

'Blind trust,' she whispered.

'Blind trust,' he confirmed. 'I've never had anyone give me unconditional trust before—never had anyone stand by me in the face of overwhelming odds. I guess it's a futile dream. Still...it's my dream.'

She sat up and slipped her arms around his neck. 'If I could wrap my trust in a box, I'd give it to you as my wedding-gift,' she told him. 'But all I have is words.'

'Don't make promises you can't keep,' he warned.

Her brows drew together and she nodded. 'Then I'll promise to try. That's the best I can offer right now.'

'It's a start.'

He cupped her face and, after what seemed an endless moment, he lowered his mouth to hers. It was as though she'd been waiting an eternity for his possession. There'd be no further reprieve, no postponing the inevitable. After tonight she'd belong to him, joined with bonds more permanent than his ring on her finger.

Champagne and strawberries flavored his kiss, a kiss he ended all too soon, leaving her desperately hungry for more. 'Hunter,' she pleaded.

'Easy,' he answered, his lips drifting the length of her jaw. 'Slow and easy, love.'

And he did take it slow, seducing her with long, deep kisses, igniting the fires that burned so hotly between them. Slipping her robe from her shoulders, he cupped the pendant that had become a permanent fixture about her neck and in silent homage his mouth found the spot between her breasts where it so often nestled.

She gripped his shoulders, her eyes falling shut, blocking out the pagan sight of his dark head against her white skin. All she could do after that was feel...feel the touch of his tongue and teeth on her breasts, feel the hard, possessive sweep of his hands as he stripped off her robe, baring her to his gaze.

'You're even more beautiful than I remember,' he told her.

'Make love to me, Hunter. Now.' She shifted in his grasp, wanting to be closer, trembling with the strength of her need.

He lowered her to the blanket and she opened her eyes, staring up at him. He held himself above her, the embodiment of lean, masculine grace and raw power—a power muted only by the tenderness reflected in the black depths of his gaze. Then he came to her, joined with her, his body a welcome weight, hard and angled and taut beneath her hands.

And there, sequestered within their tiny slice of heaven, he showed her anew the true meaning of ecstasy. She didn't hold back. She couldn't. For, if she gave him nothing else, she'd give him all the love she possessed.

They spent the entire weekend at the apartment, re-learning their roles as lovers. For Leah it deepened a love that had never truly died. Unfortunately, Hunter's reaction proved more difficult to read. He wanted her; she didn't doubt that for a minute. She could inflame him with the simplest of touches—his dark eyes burning with a hunger that stole her breath. Nor could she complain of his treatment, his gentleness revealing a certain level of caring. But love? If he experienced such an emotion, he kept it well-hidden.

To Leah's dismay, leaving the seclusion of the apartment and returning to the ranch proved to be the hardest thing she'd ever done.

Worse, the morning after their return Hunter rode Dreamseeker, the stallion at long last surrendering to the stronger, more determined force. Leah couldn't help drawing a comparison, feeling as though she, too, had surrendered to Hunter's perseverance, giving everything while he remained aloof and independent and in control. Never had she felt so defenseless, so aware of her own vulnerability—nor had she ever felt so afraid. As much as she'd have liked to protect herself, she suspected it was far too late.

The morning after Hunter broke the stallion, her fears took a new direction. Dreamseeker was missing from the pasture.

'Saddle Ladyfinger,' Hunter directed. 'And grab your slicker. It looks like more rain.'

Struggling to hide her concern, she did as he'd ordered, lashing the yellow oilskin to the back of her saddle. 'Could he have smashed down the fence again?' she asked apprehensively.

Hunter shook his head. 'Not a chance.'

He mounted his buckskin and they started out, riding toward the area the horse had broken through before. They'd almost reached the southernmost point of Hampton land when the first scream reverberated across the pasture.

Leah had heard that sound only twice before in her life, and it was one she'd never forget. It turned her blood to ice. Throwing a panicked glance in Hunter's direction, she dug her heels into Ladyfinger's flanks and charged toward the sound, Hunter at her side. Throughout the tense moments of that mad dash to the Circle P she prayed she'd be wrong. Prayed that Dreamseeker was safe.

Arriving at the property line, they paused briefly. The fence separating the two ranches had indeed been knocked down again, and Leah's heart sank. There was no doubt now as to what had happened . . . nor what was about to happen. Another scream echoed from over the next ridge, answered by an equally infuriated trumpeting. Crossing on to Circle P land, they sprinted to the top of the hill and discovered Bull Jones sitting on his mount, watching the scene below unfold.

Dreamseeker stood at one end of a small, tree-enclosed meadow, circling a chestnut thoroughbred stallion. Off to one side milled a nervous herd of mares, undoubtedly the motivation for the fight. Dreamseeker reared on to his hind legs, gnashing his teeth and striking out with his hooves. The chestnut joined in the ritualistic dance, copying each threatening move.

'You did this, Leah,' Bull growled, gimlet-eyed. 'I told you to secure your fence-line. Now it's too late. If that stallion of yours injures our thoroughbred, you'll pay big. Real big. Baby Blue's worth a fortune. If he goes down, it'll cost you your ranch.'

Leah glared at the foreman. 'You deliberately moved Baby Blue and those mares to this pasture in order to rile up our stallion. As to the fence...we reinforced it just last week. The only way Dreamseeker could have broken through is if you cut the wire.'

He laughed. 'Knowing something's one thing. Proving it is a whole different story.'

'She won't have to,' Hunter said in a clipped voice. 'I will.'

With a shrill roar, Dreamseeker reared back, then dropped to the ground with a bone-jarring thud and charged. Baby Blue, his eyes rolling back in his head, raced to meet his challenger.

'No!' Leah shrieked. Without thought or consideration of the danger, she slammed her heels into her horse's flanks, slipping and sliding down the hill.

'Leah!' she heard Hunter shout.

She ignored him, fighting to stay in the saddle while forcing her mare toward the heat of battle. Halfway down the hill, she realized that the terrified animal would go no further. Leah reined to a stop and flung herself out of the saddle. In two seconds flat she'd ripped her rain-slicker free. Screaming at the top of her lungs, she ran straight at the stallions, slapping the bright yellow oilskin in the air as hard as she could.

Just as she reached them the thoroughbred went down, and a sudden image of Hunter distracting the bull with his shirt flashed through her mind. Before Dreamseeker could move in for the kill she threw the slicker directly into her horse's face. He shied wildly, dropping his head and shaking it in an attempt to rid himself of the entrapping coat.

'Leah, move!' Hunter yelled, sprinting to her side. Clamping an arm around her waist, he threw her clear of the danger. Without a moment's hesitation he planted himself between her and imminent peril, nothing at hand with which to protect himself but his rope.

Dreamseeker bucked madly and finally succeeded in flinging the slicker off his head. He froze for an instant, as though trying to decide whether to charge the man or the downed stallion. It was all the opportunity Hunter needed. In one swift move his rope ripped through the air, snagging the stallion's forefeet. Throwing every ounce of mass and muscle behind the effort, Hunter wrenched the rope taut, dropping the horse in his tracks.

Spinning around, he ran flat out toward Leah. Snatching her to her feet with one hand, he hurled the rope around the nearest tree with the other. With more speed than artistry he secured the rope, effectively hobbling the horse.

Breathing hard, he slowly turned to face Leah. 'Woman, you and I are going to have a serious conversation. And, when it's done, your sit-down may be a little the worse for wear.'

'Are you threatening me with physical violence?' Leah asked in disbelief.

His wrath shredded his rigid control. 'You're damned right I'm threatening you with physical violence!' he bit out. 'After what you pulled you'll be lucky if that's all I threaten you with.'

'I couldn't just wait while one of those stallions killed the other!'

He towered over her, his hands clenched, a muscle leaping in his jaw. 'Oh, yes, you could have, and you damned well should have. Before this day is through I intend to explain it to you in terms you won't soon forget. For now, you have a more pressing matter to take care of.'

'What's that?'

He gestured. 'Your horse,' he said flatly.

She couldn't believe she'd been so easily side-tracked. To her relief, she saw that Baby Blue had regained his feet and abandoned the field of battle, driving his harem of mares before him. She ran toward Dreamseeker, careful to keep a safe distance. Slowly she circled the downed animal, searching for any serious damage. He lay on his side, blowing hard and trembling, but without apparent injury. Before she could decide how to handle the stallion's safe return to his pasture, Bull Jones rode up.

'Move out of the way, Leah,' he ordered furiously. She looked up, horrified to discover Bull's Remington free of his scabbard and aimed at her stallion. 'I'm gonna shoot that bronco right between the eyes. If you don't want to get hurt, you'll stand clear.'

Leah never saw Hunter move. One minute Bull sat astride his horse, the next minute he lay flat on his back, his gun thrown out of reach and Hunter's foot planted in the center of his chest.

'We never had the chance to introduce ourselves,' Hunter said in a soft, menacing voice. 'It's time to correct that oversight.'

'I don't care who you are, *hombre*. Get the hell off me and get the hell off my land.' He squirmed in the dirt, attempting to worm his way out of his predicament. Not that it did him any good. Leah could tell he'd remain where he was until Hunter decided otherwise.

'First, it's not your land.' The boot pressed a little harder. 'And second, the name's Pryde. Hunter Pryde. You call me *hombre* once more and you won't be talking—or chewing—any time soon.'

'*Pryde!*' Bull's eyes bulged. 'I know you! You're——'

'Leah's husband,' Hunter interrupted smoothly.

'Aw, shoot. I didn't know *you* were Pryde...' Bull protested. 'You shoulda said something.'

'Being a fair and reasonable man, I'm going to give you two choices. You can get up, climb on your horse, and ride out of here, nice and friendly-like, or you can stay and we'll discuss the situation further. Well, *muchacho*? What's it going to be?'

'Let me up. I'll leave.'

Hunter removed his foot and stepped back. And though he seemed relaxed—his hands at his sides, his legs slightly spread—Leah knew that he stood poised for action should Bull offer any further threat. The foreman slowly gained his feet and reached for his rifle.

'Don't bother. You won't be needing it,' Hunter said, an unmistakable warning in his voice. 'And one more thing.'

'What's that?' Bull asked warily.

'As you ride out of here, take a final, long look around.'

Understanding dawned and a heavy flush crept up Bull's neck. 'You can't do that. I have pull, you know.'

Hunter's chilly smile was empty of humor. 'I have more.'

'You haven't heard the last of this,' Bull growled, mounting up.

'Any time you want to finish the discussion, feel free to drop by. I'll be happy to accommodate you.' Hunter waited until the foreman had ridden out of earshot before switching his attention to Leah. 'Your turn.'

'How can you do that?' she demanded, gesturing toward Bull's rapidly retreating back. 'How can *you* fire him?'

Hunter's gaze became enigmatic. 'Let's just say that Buddy Peterson will find it in his best interest to follow through with my...suggestion.'

A tiny frown creased her brow. After a moment's consideration she nodded. 'Let's hope you're right.'

'I am.'

He took a step in her direction and she froze. As much as she'd have liked to run for the hills, she refused to back down. 'I know. I know. It's my turn. Well, go ahead. Yell at me some more. Stomp around and cuss if you want. Just get it over with.'

'This isn't some sort of joke, Leah.' He snatched her close, practically shaking her. 'You could have been killed. And there wouldn't have been a damned thing I could have done to prevent it. I'd never have reached you in time.'

'I had to save Dreamseeker,' she protested.

He thrust her away, as though afraid of what he might do if he continued to touch her. 'You don't get it, do you? That horse is nothing compared to your safety. I should have let Jones shoot the damned animal and be done with it.'

She caught her breath in disbelief. 'You can't be serious.'

His eyes burned with barely suppressed rage, his features set in stark, remote lines. 'I'm dead serious. You promise me here and now that you won't ever, for any reason, risk your life for that horse again, or he goes.'

He wasn't kidding. She could tell when a man had reached the end of his rope and, without question, Hunter had reached it. Slowly she nodded. 'I promise.'

'I intend to hold you to that promise,' he warned.

She twisted her hands together. 'But you won't sell Dreamseeker?'

His voice turned dry, the rage slowly dying from his eyes. 'Don't worry, Leah. Your horse is safe for now, even if you aren't. Mount up. Let's get this bronco home. And when we get there, and my temper has had a chance to cool, you and I will finish this conversation.'

'That'll be some time next week, right?' she dared to suggest.

He yanked the brim of his stetson low over his brow. 'Try next month.' And with that he headed for his horse.

Hunter placed a call to Kevin Anderson, not bothering to waste time on preliminaries. 'I fired Bull Jones today.'

Kevin swore softly. 'What do you want me to do?'

'Take care of it. Make sure there aren't any... complications.'

'Is it Leah? Has she found out?'

'No. I don't think so. But considering I gave Jones his walking papers in front of her, it'll be a miracle if she doesn't at least suspect.'

'If she does——'

'Don't worry,' Hunter interrupted sharply. 'I'll handle my wife.'

A small sound brought his head around. Leah stood at the door, looking nervous and uncertain. Had she heard? he wondered, keeping his expression impassive. He gestured for her to come in.

'Listen, I have to go, Kevin. I'll be in touch.'

He hung up, not waiting for an answer. He stood up and walked around the desk, leaning against the edge. There he stayed, silent and watchful, as she approached. Catching her braid, he tugged her close. He wanted her. God, he wanted her. And he knew without a doubt that she wanted him as well. He could see it in her eyes, in the faint trembling of her lips and the rapid pounding of her heart.

Not bothering to conceal the strength of his desire, he pulled her roughly between his legs. Her eyes widened, the color almost violet with emotion. Her breath came swiftly between her parted lips, a delicate flush tinting her cheeks. It took only a minute to unbraid her hair, spreading the silvery curls around them like a silken cloak.

Unable to resist, he kissed her, taking her softness with a desire fast flaring out of control. 'Don't fight me,' he muttered against her mouth. 'Not now. Not any more.'

'Fight you?' she said, her voice wavering between laughter and passion. 'I wish I could.'

'Then kiss me, Leah. Kiss me like you mean it.'

She seemed to melt into him. 'I've always meant it. Haven't you realized that by now?' she whispered. And, wrapping her arms around his neck, she gave herself to him.

Leah stared at the ceiling, the moon throwing a shadowed pattern of branches across the smooth surface. What had he meant? she wondered uneasily.

She turned her head and studied Hunter as he slept. His passion tonight had exceeded anything that had ever gone before. More than once she'd nearly said the words, almost told him how much she loved him. But something had held her back. His conversation with 'Kevin', perhaps?

She frowned up at the ceiling again. So what had Hunter meant? What, precisely, did 'I'll handle my wife' signify? And why did it fill her with such an overwhelming dread?

CHAPTER TEN

LEAH awoke the next morning and for the first time found herself alone in bed. She sat up in a panic, not liking the sensation of having been deserted. Hunter was right. Waking in his arms made a difference to her entire day and she didn't appreciate the abrupt change.

She got up and went in search of him, only to discover that he'd left a brief note explaining he'd been unexpectedly called to Houston. The knowledge filled her with a vague alarm. She'd hoped to talk to him, to be held by him, to be reassured that his conversation with this . . . Kevin had nothing to do with their marriage—or the ranch.

So much for blind trust, she thought with a guilty pang. Let one small incident a little out of the ordinary happen and her trust evaporated like mist before the morning sun.

'I think I'll go into town and do some shopping,' she told her grandmother, needing an outlet for her restlessness.

'Stop by the jewelers and see if my watch is fixed,' Rose requested. 'They've had it a full week and my wrist feels naked.'

'Sure thing,' Leah agreed.

Not long after, she climbed into the ranch pick-up and drove the thirty minutes to the small town of Crossroads. She spent a full hour window-shopping and indulging in an éclair at Cindy's Sinful Pastries before coming upon a new antiques store. Intrigued, she went in, and after

much diligent poking around unearthed a small statue
that she knew she'd purchase regardless of the price.

Made of pewter, a dull silver knight rode a rearing
charger. In one hand he clasped a lance, holding a fierce,
ruby-eyed dragon at bay. With his other he pulled a veiled
damsel to safety. The damsel's flowing gown reminded
Leah of her own wedding-dress and she grinned. Considering the snow crystal story he'd told her, it was
perfect. She'd put it in the study and see how long it
took Hunter to notice—and whether he caught the significance of the gesture. After paying for the statue she
crossed the street to the jewelers.

'Morning, Leah.' Clyde, the owner, greeted her, with
a familiar smile. 'I just finished Rose's repair job last
night.' He punched the charge into his register and
handed her the boxed watch. Eyeing the imprinted
shopping bag she carried, he said, 'I see you visited our
new antiques store. Find something you liked?'

'Sure did. Want to see?' At his interested nod she
carefully unwrapped her purchase, and proudly displayed it for the jeweler.

'My, that's a fine piece.' He peered at it over his wire-
rimmed spectacles. 'A belated wedding-gift?' he asked,
with the presumptuousness of a lifelong friendship. At
her shy acknowledgement he beamed. 'I'm glad.
Hunter's a good man.'

A sudden idea occurred to her and she pulled Hunter's
pendant from beneath her blouse. 'Clyde... Can you
make a miniature of this?'

'To go around the knight's neck?' he guessed. His
mouth puckered in a thoughtful frown. 'Shouldn't be
too difficult. Actually, I have a stone that would be ideal.'

'How long would it take?' she asked anxiously.

His eyes twinkled with amusement. 'I think Mrs Whitehaven's ring adjustment can wait. How does an hour sound?'

She sighed in relief. 'It sounds ideal.'

'And if I can make one small suggestion?' He crossed to a display of pewter charms and removed one of the larger pieces—a cowboy hat. It fit the knight as though made for him. 'I could snip off the link and smooth it down, fix it to the knight's head so it won't come off. What do you think?'

It was perfect. 'Do it,' she directed. 'I'll be back in an hour. And Clyde?' He glanced up from the statue and she grinned. 'Thanks.'

'Any time, Leah. Any time.'

Precisely sixty minutes later she left the jewelers for the second time, her statue—complete with cowboy hat and pendant—gift-wrapped and safely tucked away in her handbag. To her dismay, the first person she ran into was Bull Jones. Before she could evade him, he blocked her path.

'Why, if it isn't Miz Hampton.' He removed his cigar from between his teeth. 'Oh, excuse me. That's Mrs Pryde, isn't it?'

'Yes, it is,' she retorted sharply. 'If you were smart, you'd remember that and stay clear, before Hunter hears you've been bothering me again.'

'I'm not worried. Your husband isn't here. And by the time he returns, I'll be long gone.'

Her blood ran cold and she glanced around, reassured to see that their confrontation had witnesses. She glared at Bull. 'You have something to say to me? Then say it. Otherwise, move out of my way before I bring the whole town down around your ears.'

'You always were a feisty little shrew. Okay. Why beat around the bush? Your husband's in Houston, isn't he?' He laughed at her expression. 'What, nothing to say? Aren't you even going to ask how I know?'

'I couldn't care less.' She refused to play into this man's hands. Not that it stopped him.

'I'll tell you anyway,' he offered with mock generosity. 'He's there because he's called the Lyon Enterprises' board together.'

She shrugged indifferently. 'He knows the board. That's not news to me,' she claimed.

But Bull shook his head. 'He doesn't just know the board. He *runs* the board.'

She jerked as though slapped. 'What are you talking about?' she demanded.

'That got your attention, didn't it?' He laughed, the sound hard-edged and rough. 'Hunter Pryde *is* Lyon Enterprises. Course I didn't find that out until he had me fired.'

'I don't believe you.'

'Suit yourself. But think about it.' His cigar jabbed the air, making small smoky punctuation marks. 'Lyon...Pryde...the Circle *P*. It all fits. And if you wanted to confirm it, it'd be easy enough to check out.'

'How?' The question was dragged from her.

'Call Lyon Enterprises. Ask for Pryde's office. If he has one there, you'll have your answer. You'll know he married you to get his hands on your ranch.'

'All I'll know is that he has an office,' she said scornfully. 'That doesn't mean he owns Lyon Enterprises. Nor does it mean he married me to get the ranch.' She wondered if he heard the edge of desperation in her voice. Probably.

'He owns it,' Bull said with absolute confidence. 'And when he realized he couldn't buy you out or force you out, he married you.'

She had to leave. She wouldn't stand here and be poisoned by any more of this man's filth. 'Get away from me, Jones. I'm not listening to you.' She attempted to push past him, but he grabbed her arm and jerked her to a stop.

He spoke fast, his words striking with a deadly accuracy. 'You were all set to marry some joe so that you wouldn't lose your spread. If you had, Lyon would have been permanently blocked. The second Pryde heard about it, he shows up, and marries you himself. Pretty shrewd move. He gets the girl and the land without paying one red cent.'

'I still own the ranch, not Hunter.'

'Do you?' He leaned closer and she turned her head away in revulsion. 'Maybe you do now. But for how much longer? Those business types will find a way around that little problem. They always do. And then you and your granny will be out on your collective backsides.'

With that he released her and, clamping his cigar between his teeth, walked away. She stood in the middle of the sidewalk for an endless moment. Then she practically ran to the truck. Sitting safely in the cab, she gripped the steering-wheel as though her life depended on it, struggling for a measure of calm.

Putting the conversation into perspective, she knew Bull had an ax to grind and so she needed to weigh his comments accordingly. But what horrified her so was that every word he had uttered made perfect sense, playing on her most intrinsic fears. Hunter *had* wanted the ranch above all else. And never once had he been willing to tell her why.

Because he knew she'd never marry him if he did?

She stared blindly out the front windshield for several minutes. She had to think, had to keep a clear head. Either Bull spoke the truth or he lied. It was that simple. All she had to do was figure out which.

Conrad Michaels. The name came to her from nowhere and she seized it with relief. Of course! He had contacts. He could do some digging...off the record. Without giving it further consideration, she started the engine and pointed the truck in the direction of home. She'd call Conrad. He'd help her.

So much for blind trust, she thought in anguish. But how could she be expected to trust when her knight had suddenly turned back into the dragon?

Leah took a deep breath and spoke brightly into the phone, 'Conrad? It's Leah. I'm fine, thanks. And you?' She listened for several minutes while he told her, then admitted, 'Yes, I did call for a reason. I was curious about something and thought you could help.'

'Of course, Leah,' Conrad said agreeably enough. 'What can I do for you?'

She tapped her pencil against the desk blotter. 'It's...it's about our loan. The ranch loan. Did Hunter arrange for it with your bank? I mean... You had the old one and I thought...'

'It's not with our bank,' Conrad informed her bluntly. 'Not any more. Your lawyer insisted that Hunter initially place it with us as part of your prenuptial agreement. But I heard that shortly after your marriage it was bought out by an independent concern. All perfectly legal, you understand.'

'But it was with you originally?'

'Yes.'

Now for the hard part. After a brief pause, she asked, 'Do you know who bought it out?'

'What's this about, Leah? Why aren't you asking Hunter these questions?'

She heard the tension in his voice and regretted putting him in such an uncomfortable position. Unfortunately, she had to know. 'I'm asking you, Connie,' she said evenly, deliberately used the family nickname. 'I need to make sure the payments are current, that I'm not in arrears.'

'I see.' He sounded old and tired.

She closed her eyes, hating herself for involving him. But there'd been no one else she could turn to. 'I realize you're retired and out of the loop. Still, I'd hoped you'd have contacts who could give you the information. I'm sorry to ask for such a big favor. I wouldn't, unless it was important,' she apologized.

'Of course. I'll look into it.'

'You'll be discreet?'

'Don't worry. I'll be discreet.'

She thanked him and hung up, checking his name off the list she'd composed. One down. Studying the piece of paper in front of her, she eyed the second name and number. This next would take even more nerve. She forced herself to reach for the phone again and dial the number. An operator answered almost immediately.

'Lyon Enterprises. How may I direct your call?'

'Hunter Pryde, please.'

'One moment.'

After a brief delay a secretary answered. 'Felicia Carter speaking. May I help you?'

Leah frowned. 'I'm sorry. I asked for Hunter Pryde's office.'

'I can help you,' the secretary hastened to assure. 'May I ask who's calling?'

'Is he in?' Leah persisted.

'He's tied up with the board all day. I can give him a message if you'd like.'

Leah closed her eyes. 'No message.' She started to hang up, then froze. 'Wait! His title. Could you tell me his title with the company?'

'I'm afraid you'll have to discuss that with Mr Pryde.' A hint of suspicion tinged Felicia's voice. 'Could I have your name, please?'

Without another word, Leah cradled the receiver. So. Part of Bull's story checked out. Hunter could be reached at Lyon Enterprises. But that didn't mean he had an office there; it didn't even mean he worked there. And it was far from indisputable evidence that he owned the company. There's no need to panic, she told herself, breathing a little easier. She'd managed to glean two facts. He had business in Houston with Lyon and their meeting was ongoing.

Beneath her hand the phone rang and she lifted it. 'Yes? Hello?'

'It's Conrad.'

From the reluctance in his voice she could tell that she wouldn't appreciate the information he'd gathered. 'Get it over with. I can take it,' she told him.

'It's not anything definitive,' he was quick to explain, 'so don't jump to any conclusions. The company that bought out your note is named HP, Inc.'

'HP, Inc? As in... Hunter Pryde, Incorporated?'

'It's...possible, I suppose. I couldn't get the status of the loan itself. But I have their number in Houston, if you want it.'

'I want it.' She jotted down the information and thanked him.

'Let me know if you need me,' Conrad said. 'I had hoped...' He didn't finish his sentence. He didn't have to.

'Me, too,' she said in a soft voice.

This time she didn't delay placing the call. Asking for Hunter's office, the operator once again put her through, and once again a secretary offered to take a message.

'This is Felicia Carter at Lyon Enterprises,' Leah said. 'I'm trying to track down Mr Pryde.'

'Why... I believe he's working over there today, Ms Carter.'

Leah managed a careless laugh. 'How silly of me. I must have gotten my days mixed up.' Then on impulse she said, 'I don't know how he keeps it straight. It must be difficult owning two such large companies.'

'Yes, it is. But Mr Pryde's an unusual man. And he only hires the best. Delegation. It makes his life much easier. One minute, please.' Leah could hear a brief, muffled conversation before the secretary came back on the line. 'Mr Pryde's assistant just came in. Would you like to speak to him?'

'Kevin?' she asked casually.

'Oh, you know him?'

She ducked the question. 'That won't be necessary. I'll get the information I need at this end.' To her horror, her voice broke. 'Thank you for your help,' she managed to say, and hung up.

The tears, once started, couldn't be stopped. She despised herself for being so weak. It wasn't the end of all her dreams. She still had her grandmother and the ranch. She still had her employees and Dreamseeker. But somehow it wasn't enough. She wanted Hunter. Most of all, she wanted Hunter's love.

Too bad all Hunter wanted was her ranch.

'What's going on, Leah?'

Leah looked up, distressed to see her grandmother standing in the doorway. Silently she shook her head, swiping at her damp cheeks and struggling to bring her emotions under control.

'Is it Hunter?' Rose asked, stepping into the room. 'Has something happened to him?'

'No! Yes!' Leah covered her face with her hands, fighting to maintain control. She couldn't afford to break down again. 'His health is fine, if that's what you mean.'

Rose crossed to the desk. 'Then, what's wrong?'

'Hunter owns Lyon Enterprises, that's what's wrong.' She slumped in the chair. 'I'm…I'm sorry. I didn't mean to blurt it out like that.'

'Hunter owns Lyon Enterprises,' Rose repeated. 'You're joking.'

'It's true,' Leah said in a tired voice. 'I just got off the phone with his office. Dammit! What am I going to do?'

'You're going to talk to him, of course.'

'*Talk*?' She stared at her grandmother in disbelief. 'What's to say? "Oh, by the way, did you really marry me just to get your hands on my ranch?" That's why he proposed. He never made any secret of the fact.'

Rose planted her hands on her hips. 'Then why act so betrayed?' she snapped. 'What's the difference if he wanted the ranch for himself or for his business? If you married the owner of Lyon Enterprises it sounds to me like you were the one to get the better end of that deal.'

That brought her up short. 'Excuse me?'

'You heard me. Think about it. Hunter's gotten one thing out of this so-called bargain—a lot of hard work and darned little thanks. But if he's Lyon, you get the ranch, the Circle P, and anything else he cares to throw into the hat...' She cackled. 'Best of all, you get Hunter. Yessir. Sounds like a damned good trade to me.'

'Until he manages to obtain title to the ranch and forecloses on us. Next comes the divorce and then we're begging on the streets.'

Rose snorted. 'You really are a ninny. Get your butt out of that chair, climb into the pick-up and drive to Houston. Talk to the man. Ask him why he married you. Flat out.'

'I already know——'

'He actually told you he married you for the ranch?' Rose asked with raised eyebrows. 'Or did you assume it?'

Leah shook her head in bewilderment. 'I don't remember. I...I don't think he said. Every time I asked, he'd just stand there.'

'Looking insulted, maybe? I would have.'

'Why?' she demanded. 'That's the reason we married. It's not a secret. No matter how much you try to wrap it up in pretty ribbons and bows, I married for business, not love. And so did Hunter.'

'I'm sure you're right. A man as rich as Croesus, as smart as a whip and as handsome as ever came down the pike is going to sacrifice himself in marriage in order to get his hands on one little old Texas ranch.' She heaved a sigh. 'Sounds reasonable to me.'

Leah bit down on her lip. 'Stop making so much sense! You're confusing me.'

'Good. Now for the punchline. Do you love him?'

There was only one possible answer to that question. 'Yes,' she said without a moment's hesitation. 'More than anything.'

Her grandmother grinned. 'That's all you need to remember. Here's your purse. Here's the keys to the pick-up. Go to Houston. I'll see you tomorrow. Or the next day. Or the one after that. Go hide out in that apartment of Hunter's and make some babies. I want to be a great-grandma. Soon. You hear me, girl?'

'I hear you. Judging by how loud you're shouting I'm sure Inez, her children and at least two-thirds of our wranglers heard you, too.'

But she obeyed. Without another word of argument, Leah took the keys and her purse and walked out of the study. Not giving herself a chance to reconsider and chicken out, she climbed into the pick-up and started the engine. Pulling a Bull Jones, she spun the wheel and stomped on the gas, kicking up an impressive rooster tail of dirt and gravel as she headed down the drive.

Half a dozen times she almost turned back. But something kept her going. One way or another she'd have her answers—whether she liked them or not. And maybe—just maybe—she could convince Hunter to give their marriage a chance. A real chance. She loved him. And she intended to fight for that love.

She only got lost twice, but the delay added to her growing tension. Finally she found the Lyon Enterprises building and pulled into the underground garage. She didn't know how she'd talk her way into the board meeting, but somehow she'd do it. Stopping at the security desk, she showed her credentials.

'Leah Pryde,' she told the guard. 'Mrs Hunter Pryde. I'm supposed to meet my husband.'

'Certainly, Mrs Pryde. I'll ring upstairs and let him know you're here.'

'I'd rather you didn't,' she said, offering her most persuasive smile. 'I'd like to surprise him.'

He looked momentarily uncertain, then nodded. 'Sure. I suppose that would be all right.'

'Thanks.'

With a calm that she was far from feeling she walked to the bank of elevators, and all too soon arrived on the executive floor. This time no secretary waited to greet her. She glanced down at her clothes and wished she'd thought to change before leaving home. Jeans and a cotton blouse didn't seem quite appropriate. Did they have dress codes on executive floors? At the very least she should have brushed her hair. Her braid was almost nonexistent, loose curls drifting into her face.

She peeked up and down the deserted hallway, aware that it wouldn't be wise to delay much longer. Someone would soon stop her and she didn't doubt for a minute that they'd call security or, worse... Hunter. Looking neither right nor left, she started for the boardroom. If she was going to get thrown out of the place, she'd rather have done something to earn it.

Five yards from the huge double doors, the first road-block appeared. 'Excuse me,' the tall, perfectly groomed woman said. 'May I help you?'

'No,' Leah replied and kept walking.

The persistent woman scooted ahead, planting herself square in front of the boardroom doors. 'I'm Felicia Carter,' she tried again, offering her hand. 'And you are?'

'Late. Excuse me.' Leah brushed past the secretary and reached for the door, but Felicia proved too quick. The woman grasped Leah's hand and shook it.

'It's a pleasure, Miss...?'

'Leah.'

'Leah.' The handshake turned to an iron-like clasp. 'If you'd come this way, we can find out what your situation is and we can get it taken care of right away.'

'*We* appreciate your help,' Leah said with an amiable smile, and turned in the direction Felicia indicated. The second the woman moved from the door Leah broke free, and lunged for the knob. An instant later she scooted inside the boardroom and slammed the huge door in Felicia's face, locking it.

'Take care of that,' she muttered beneath her breath, and turned to face the board members.

To her horror there were about twice the number there'd been on her last visit. And every last one of them stared at her as though she'd just pulled up in a flying saucer. At the far end, where Buddy Peterson had last been, sat Hunter, his chair pushed back, his feet propped on the glass table. Buddy now sat to Hunter's right.

'Don't be shy.' Hunter's words, gentle and yet oddly menacing, dropped into the deafening silence. 'Come on in.'

'Okay.' She took a single step forward. 'I think that's far enough.'

For an endless minute their gazes met and held—and if his was implacably black and remote, she didn't doubt for an instant that hers was filled with a mixture of defiance and fear.

The phone at Hunter's elbow emitted a muted beep and he picked it up. 'Yes, Felicia, she's here. Relax. I'll take care of it.' He hung up and addressed the board members. 'Ladies. Gentlemen. My wife.' Cautious murmurs of greeting drifted around the room and after a long, tense moment, he asked, 'What can we do for you, Leah?'

She swallowed hard. Maybe she should have rehearsed this part at some point during the drive. She glanced at him uncertainly. 'I wondered...' She took a deep breath. 'I wondered if there was something you have to tell me.'

His eyes narrowed and he removed his feet from the table and straightened in his chair. 'No. Is there something you have to tell me?'

So, he wasn't going to admit who he really was. He'd warned her that he'd never explain himself again. Still, he had to know that she wouldn't be here if she didn't at least suspect the truth. He had to know that the cards were stacked against him. And yet he expected her to trust him...or not. It was that simple. And suddenly she realized that despite everything she'd been told, despite all the facts that proved his duplicity, she did trust him. And she loved him.

'No,' she whispered. 'I don't have anything to tell you.'

His mouth tightened. 'Then if you'd excuse us?'

With a passion that brought tears to her eyes she wished she'd never come, that she'd never listened to Bull Jones, that she'd never given an ounce of weight to any of the despicable suggestions he'd made. Did she believe Jones more than Hunter? Never. Now she'd failed. She'd failed her husband, and she'd failed herself. When it came to a choice, she'd chosen to doubt him. And he'd never forgive her for that.

Her shoulders sagged in defeat and she started to turn away. Then she froze. What had he said that night at his apartment? 'I've never had anyone give me unconditional trust before—never had anyone stand by me in the face of overwhelming odds. I guess it's a futile dream. Still...it's my dream.'

She set her jaw. No. She wouldn't walk away. She wouldn't give up. She loved him. She loved him more than anything in her life. More than Dreamseeker, more than her employees, even more than the damned ranch. He wanted blind trust? Fine. She'd give it to him.

'Yes,' she said, turning around again. 'I do have something to say. In private, if you don't mind.'

'Ladies, gentlemen. Sign the papers,' Hunter ordered, snapping his briefcase closed and lifting it from the table. 'If you'll excuse us. My wife and I have a few matters to discuss in private.' He stood and walked to a door that opened on to a small office off the conference-room. Shutting them in the restrictive confines, he tossed his briefcase on to the desk and turned to her. 'What the hell is this about, Leah?'

She gathered her nerve to speak, to say the words that were long, long overdue. 'The whole time we've been married you've asked for only one thing from me. You told me that it's more precious to you than anything else. I offered to box it up for a wedding-gift if I could. Well... Here it is. My gift to you. It's up to you what you do with it.' She opened her purse and pulled out the gift-box from the jewelers.

He stared at it, making no move to take what she offered. 'What is it?'

'Open it and find out.'

He took the box then, and ripped it apart, removing the statue. She heard the swift intake of his breath, saw the lines of his jaw tighten. And then he looked at her, his black eyes aflame with a fierce, raw joy. 'Do you mean this?' he demanded. 'You trust me?'

She nodded, biting down on her lip. 'With all my heart.'

A brief knock sounded at the door and Buddy Peterson stuck his head in the office. 'Papers are signed and the boardroom's all yours. By the way, that was a gutsy move. Some might call it chivalrous. You could have lost everything you own.'

Hunter inclined his head in acknowledgement. 'Instead I won.' He glanced at Leah. 'Everything.'

Buddy grinned. 'I guess things will change now that you own the whole shooting-match.'

'Count on it,' Hunter agreed.

The door closed behind the executive and they were alone again. 'I don't understand,' she whispered. 'I thought you already owned Lyon Enterprises.'

He shook his head. 'Not until two minutes ago.'

'And before that?'

'I was their chief rival... and their worst nightmare.'

She could hardly take it in. 'Why didn't you tell me?'

'Because until the papers were signed there was nothing to tell. Like the man said, I could have failed in my takeover bid and lost everything.'

'Not everything,' she suddenly realized, tears starting to her eyes. 'Not the ranch.'

'No,' he conceded. 'I made sure that was protected by our prenuptial agreement.'

'You told me to read it. I guess I should have.' She gazed up at him a little uncertainly. 'Hunter?'

His eyes glittered with amusement. 'Yes, Leah? Could it be there's something you forgot to tell me after all?' He reached for her braid, releasing the strands and draping the curls across her shoulders.

'I believe there is.' A slow smile crept across her mouth and she tilted her head to one side. 'Yes, now that I think about it, I'm positive there is.' She stepped into his arms and rested her cheek against his chest. 'Have I told you yet how much I love you?'

He dragged the air into his lungs, releasing his breath in a long, gusty sigh. 'No. I believe you forgot to mention that part.'

'I have another question, and this time you have to answer,' she said, pulling back to look up at him. 'Why did you marry me?'

He didn't hesitate. 'Because you were going to marry the next man who walked through your door. And I couldn't let you do that unless I was that next man.' His tone reflected his determination. 'Fact is, I planned to be the only man to walk through your door.'

'But you wanted to buy the ranch.' It wasn't a question.

'True. At first, I wanted it in order to block Lyon and force them into a vulnerable position. Later it was so that I could protect you from them.'

'That's what Buddy Peterson meant when he said that the takeover attempt was a chivalrous move?'

Hunter shook his head. 'It wasn't. Buying the ranch would have facilitated my takeover. Marrying you...'

'Was riskier?' she guessed.

'A little. But worth it.' He reached behind her and removed a file folder from his briefcase, handing it to her.

'What's this?'

'Open it and find out,' he said, throwing her own words back at her.

She flipped open the file. Inside she found the deed to Hampton Homestead—free and clear, and in her name. The date on the title was the day before their wedding. 'Hunter...' she whispered.

'I love you, Leah. I've always loved you. How could I not? You've given me my dream.'

She managed a wobbly smile, tears clinging to her lashes. 'I think it's time for some new dreams, don't you?'

He enfolded her in his arms. 'Only if they're made with you,' he said.

And he kissed her. He kissed her with a love and passion that she couldn't mistake. And wrapped in his embrace she knew she'd found her life, her heart and her soul. She'd found her knight in shining armor.

At long last her dragon had been vanquished.

EPILOGUE

LEAH took a sip of coffee as she leafed through the morning paper. And then she saw it—the ad practically jumping off the page at her.

WIFE WANTED!
Male rancher in immediate and desperate need of his woman! Interested applicant should:

1. *Be 27 today and have eyes the color of Texas bluebonnets—a feisty and ornery personality is a plus!*
2. *Have extensive ranching background—and the good sense to know when not to use it!*
3. *Have solid business know-how—particularly the ability to dampen the tempers of bullheaded board members.*
4. *Be pregnant. Did I mention the doctor called?*

I am a thirty-four-year-old man and can offer you a comfortable bed and an occasional rooftop picnic with all the stars a Texas sky can hold. (Details of a more intimate nature are open to negotiation as soon as you hightail it upstairs). Your husband awaits. Impatiently!

Tossing the ad to one side, Leah leapt from her chair and ran...ran to her husband, the love of her life...but, most important of all, to the father of her baby.